Lily Trotter

The Medal of Scalon

BY MARK PETER EVANS

Order this book online at www.trafford.com
or email orders@trafford.com

Most Trafford titles are also available at major online book retailers.

Print information available on the last page.

ISBN: 978-1-4669-2021-7 (sc)
ISBN: 978-1-4669-2022-4 (hc)
ISBN: 978-1-4669-2023-1 (e)

Library of Congress Control Number: 2016905344

Trafford rev.   03/30/2016

www.trafford.com
North America & international
toll-free: 1 888 232 4444 (USA & Canada)
fax: 812 355 4082

Chapter 1

—⟋ⱳ⟍—

Darkness fell just as quick as raindrops falling from thunders of plenty.

It was Thursday July the 22nd 1832, the scare was still a distant memory and closing his eyes with the thought of peaceful sleep was just a hope in his mind; after three long hours, sleep had crept itself upon and within the bed he lay.

Hours had passed and with opening eyes his story began.

It was a glorious morning, its sun shone beams of illuminating lights throughout the great halls, and back off the walls of Temple Bury Elementary Mansion.

With its broken, rustic, stained glass windows warmed, its rays were like mellow days and times that would not be forgotten, the sort that are spent lazing and hazing as you think of the bond you share and care for loved ones, this was not the case for Todd Amati, the local priest of the chapel within the village of Black Slate. He had 'survived', but why was he left to live, his body still felt the marks from their teeth of terror cascading like a storm.

In his mind all that could be remembered was that unleashed terror, embossed in the last five days by the Lipids, that demonic clan of unearthly Werewolverine warriors who fed on fresh flesh and broken bones, an image that would petrify horror into itself, a clan that could not be broken by the four of braveness, a special band of shadow ghosts each with a distinctive name, Jamaica, Leitrim, Banter, and Blanco. These band of four braves were the peacekeepers of Black Slate but all hope had perished in this once vibrant village as the four of them were captured by the Lipids, and trapped within the oracle glass bottle of Sarnia, a mystical demon from the Aslant Mountains unseen for centuries but approached by none, one that had a mysterious hobby of collecting all shaped bottles to capture anyone with her evil magic!! Todd could still hear their screams and the torture terror that black clouded and rained blood six months previous! Burnt out corpses some of which were half eaten, bits of stench flesh and curded blood were scattered amongst the dying grass verges and broken branches from the Akko Trees, once planted to add some extra greenery to the shabby roads not that it mattered or made much of a difference now.

Decapitated bodies were strewn all over this once humble place; every living thing in this village had perished!

Casting his mind back Priest Todd remembered the day as if was yesterday, for him he lived it every hour of every day.

Things were as normal as could be, the village folk were carrying on with their daily lives, birds were singing within the tree tops on this Sunday morning the time was 9.35am!!

"Good morning," spoke Todd to the oncoming Miss Blackberry, Rose being her first name. "I see you are taking little Jessica down to the brook to sail her makeshift boat."

Little Jessica her daughter gave out such a sweet smile.

"Oh yes, Father Todd, I am," Rose replied, "it's such a lovely day and I wanted her to see if it sails, after all she has spent a lot of time making it.".

"Will you be at the morning service?" asked Father Todd.

In reply Rose said, "Don't worry, we will both be at the service, all Jessica wants to do is have a quick try and then we can come back later if it sails!"

"Well, fingers crossed it sails from one end to the other," Father Todd replied

"What time will the Chapel bell ringing be commencing today?" shouted David Marcy from across the jagged and worn pebbled road that ran down near the old store. He was the father of Blue and Danny Marcy two young blacksmiths who were given the key job of shoeing the village horses. All of the villagers had huge respect for the family, as they never asked for payment for the services they did, many of the village folk cooked fulsome meals for the three of them, to repay the kindness from them, some even thought that they were a little weird.

"Eleven past the hour," shouted back Father Todd.

"Ok thanks, I will make sure that me and the boys come to it. We will see you there then."

"You will indeed," replied Father Todd as he walked on and closed in on the Chapel…

"Clarence, come here NOW he heard a voice shout! You naughty horse, come here!!"

Father Todd raised a smile he was looking over towards where the old corner store was; one apple, two apples, three apples, maybe even more than that were being chomped from inside wooden buckets filled with spider-less cobwebs which had been left on display outside. This dumb horse's owner, Trinity Mayflower, was walking over with a set of leather reins in her hand, she was shaking her head.

"You naughty horse, you know you are not supposed to leave the stable!"

Trinity was the local elementary school mistress, not that she had many pupils Twenty three in total and the classes she ran only happened on Mondays, Wednesdays, and a Friday afternoon! She glanced over and raised a hand to Todd pointed at Clarence and threw her eyes upwards! Todd sniggered and raised his hand in reply to her!! Trinity walked over half way, with one eye on Todd and the other on her damned horse. "Looks like I can't make it to the service this morning," she called over. "I will try my best, is that OK, Father Todd? I have so much to do."

"…don't worry, Trinity, I understand. I will still see you for the special service on Tuesday instead wont I?" replied Father Todd.

"Oh yes I will be there," she said again.

"Don't forget to bring plenty of Miss Crumple's cake over," he smiled nodding his head to her.

Trinity thought. Yes ok I will bring some cakes.

Miss crumples made the greatest of cakes. but was a bit of a loner and did not like many people visiting her; she had one eye of many colours and one eye that forever blinked, breasts as big as air balloons, yellow hair and pointed ears. She used to own the sorry looking store many years ago, until old age preyed upon her. She was seen by many in the village to be very strange some even questioned her true age; some said 85 others reckoned 109, however, peace is what she wanted and Trinity was one of the select few to grace her crumpled sandstone cottage.

"Bye for now," Trinity walked over, grabbing Clarence by his mane and putting the rest of the reins over his head. She led him around the corner and towards her home and the shackled stables next door.

Tears started to roll down Father Todd's face as he closed his eyes in remembrance! They were happy times! He opened his eyes and looked at the village: emptiness, coldness and silence echoed, even the once thriving flower beds had become dried out pieces of wasteful twigs; most of the buildings were half reduced to rubble! Thirty seven graves had to be dug out by him and with every prayer he looked to the skies!

Three days of hard sweat and tears, stomach churning smells, the appearance of the odd blood blister, it took him to lay all his friends to rest, some he did not want to think about, as their terror was the worst… he felt a coward why did he hide inside the chapel when the attack began.

Why did he welcome them into the village he had brought death upon everyone. It was hard to forget if only he had known! THEM DAMNED LIPIDS. He did not even want to think of how it had become to happen all that he wanted was to forget! He could not, he knew that when the six monthly full moon appeared that's when the worst thoughts would come back to haunt! Was his life worth living he often thought?

Father Todd knew that he would have to conjure up all of his courage over the next week, as there was a full moon due to dance from the sky, it would bear itself through the nighttime's clouds and give him unholy vortices of spleen dreams, the type of ones that would send him into a bigger deeper frenzy torture, hot sweats, racing heart palpitations and bodychanging screams….

A decision had to be made by him. One that he had thought about for weeks, one that he had to accept. There was nothing left in the village. he would have to try and leave the past behind as hard as it was, hours, not minutes had ticked away from his old silver square pocket watch… Todd's decision was hard but it was settled within his mind.

He had decided to travel and board a ship to sail across to the Three Islands of Justice, and visit an old friend he had known since childhood. Tilde was her name, she was the one who had once lived in the village but was ousted out because of her black magic connections. Tilde had grey and red tangled up hair, a pointed nose and a cleft mouth and she was one who dabbled in the ways of the untrue angelicas – these were vampires of the nitric clan; hopefully she could mix up an elixir potion to try and curb his torments he thought' all that he could do was try!

The trip itself would last two days. He knew only a few rags had to be bound in an old linen cloth sack, along with a golden purple-headed flower one of five in existence, too, which Father Todd had to collect from the Gen Spirit Hills, this flower attained the power of everlasting spells to whoever wore it, something that Tilde had wanted for a vast time which would add to her weird collection of magical belongings and gain her more status within the temple of the supine dragon people. Father Todd knew that time was against him and the ship would be ready to set sail mid-afternoon on the same day, this was the only form of transportation that he could use apart from the dragon sky worms that could be called upon by blowing on the heparin horn, however he did not and could not travel this way as he would have to purchase the horn from the heckle rats, who lived in the old trees in the fields over from the village.

He knew his swiftness would have to come into play if he was to get himself aboard in time for the ship's captain 'Inertia'! This captain was a ruthless vagabond, half elfin, half vampire, not to be messed with in any way; some say he was once a gallant swordsman of the high seas until a spell had been spun upon him by the sea serpent Igauss, she was half human but had a body of a crinoline octopus and was a sea demon from the high seas, many ships and crews had perished by her hands. She only surfaced every twenty five years to feed upon, curse, and capture the souls of the good. Such is that the ship's name matched its captain, *The Vile Jewel* this ship was tall and lengthy in build, it had a treble mast and its cladding was rich in gilded silver and black-flecked armour, its insignia was a nine-winged serpent which bore four horns and would put the wily nil's up anyone who cast eyes over it. Or so the stories had been told.

Back at the run down village and walking over to his broken down cottage, Father Todd began to get ready for the journey. He packed some bits of food and rammed his stuff together inside a cloth sack knowing he had one last stop to make along the way before walking to shore's end.

Chapter 2

Treading outwards and with hand firmly clasped upon his cottage's doorknob, brazened in age cracks he turned its movement anti-clockwise to close it shut. With the cloth sack and some ancient parchments safely tucked inside, he was now ready for his walk to begin. Every few steps he would glance back at the village until it had become a shadow.

About one hour and twenty minutes it would take to reach the destination of the Gene Spirit Hills, there he would retrieve Tilde's flower, how was he going to get that prized flower? So many souls had met their fate trying in the past; he was sure that by the time he reached the hills he would figure something out.

Fifty-five minutes had passed by, he knew this as he pulled his rusty crusty pocket watch out from the his dirty and holed trousers and looked at it; he was now nearing brocket forest well not really a forest anymore its age could be seen clearly, its trees ripe with brown slick mud, leaves filled half of red death and branches that looked like long boneless arms. As he neared and started walking through it Father Todd heard a large shriek,

"Hey there!!!"

"Over here!!!"

"Can't you see me?" the voice bellowed.

Father Todd looked left, right, turned around, but could see nothing.

For a split second imagination crept into his head, was he hearing things or was a little tiredness playing its game upon him just then?

"You blind? Surely you can see me, over here, in front of you, sitting on the twisted branches above you."

Looking up Father Todd could see a smallish looking creature with a yellow face, big hands, and clawed feet, with a belly that would match and catch many a gallon of ale. It was staring down at him.

"Oh you can see me then; let me introduce myself, my name is Canting Will Fore the only tree goblin that lives in these parts! And before yourself, sir, passes through my invisible door, laden my hand with a piece of golden contraband."

"YES I have noticed you now," uttered Father Todd, "and I see no invisible door, only one shabby, gabby encrusted tree that needs a good watering in nature!"

Chuckling, Canting replied, "Well, you won't see it stupid, that's why it's invisible."

"Where is my piece of gold?" Canting said.

"How dare you ask for such things; I won't part with anything. I have no gold certainly not, never in a month of Sundays, games are not in my lane and as a Father of Heavens gates and traits I uphold the laws of non-gamblers!'

Canting frowned mysteriously, "OK, sir, and what is your name and what makes you so different not to participate in my game?"

My name is Father Todd Amati and I am travelling to retrieve a flower from the Gene Spirit Hills, then I will further my trip onwards to shore's end."

"Gene Spirit Hills? Ha-ha, you will never get to the top of them, never; there have been many clever beings tried and died in vain," expressed Canting, "however I can travel along and in song participate in your venture for a price, sir..."

"Is that what you do to everyone, expect a payment? I have just met you, and err," said Father Todd, "now…is not a good time to be taking strangers with me and besides I have nothing that you could possibly want."

With eyebrows raised, Canting tapped his long bony fingers against one of the branches and replied with, "We may have just met how else do you think you are going to get what you want? I expect some sort of payment if I am going to help you, and what about them parchments that you carry with you?"

"They are just old parts of written text that found their way into my possession many years ago. And something I hold to remind me of the village where I used to live; worthless really, but you are welcome to take a look," replied Father Todd.

"Ah…"

Jumping down, all two foot of him, Canting held out his big hands, "Hand one over then."

"Let me be the judge of that."

At first scepticism started to work its way into Father Todd's mind.

"Come on, come on," hastily spoke Canting.

"Hold on there; you go take a look and you will see their worthlessness," Father Todd said, handing one over. In a quieter, subdued voice he added, "Be extra careful with it, the paper is four hundred years old…"

"Oh I will indeed, you wait here whilst I go and sit over there upon that rock and read what is written upon it," Canting said with excitement.

Carefully opening the folded corners Canting opened the old relic of parchment up and started to read its contents:

"I Mountains my Verses and all the Ancient Dragon dusts Unravel;

I Time boundary these words and all is Unravel again.

(I Oceans across I Mystery you up inside my Enigma.)

The Corrupt Worlds go flickering out in Detective and Vampire,

And Werewolf Wand Females in:

I Humanity my Magic and all the Bracelet cross Stream Of Hearth's Smoke Ghost.

I Armoured that you Candle of Flambéed me into Nature And Romance me Human, Come dyed me quite Ghost.

(I Oceans across I Mystery you up inside my Enigma.)

Angelic arrow Blues from the Music, Arrow of Life's River Abbey's Green:

Hope Earth and Fire's Wind:

I Humanity my Magic and all the Bracelet cross Stream Of Hearts' Smoke Ghost.

I Prophesied you'd braveness Of Four the way you Elements Purple,

But I Voyage Heaven and I Underground your Water.

(I Oceans across I Mystery you up inside my Enigma.) I should have Snow angelic an Element of Save instead; At least when Burning desires they Old back again.

I Humanity my Magic and all the Bracelet cross Stream Of Hearts' Smoke Ghost."

Canting looked up towards Father Todd and as he handed it back he said, "Where did you get this from?",

"Why do you ask? I stated that they were just old bits of text."

"Oh, oh, smiling with happily chirpily creatures lips, well in the text I have read it is a song that has magical words. It's not a spell, but more powerful than any contraband and I will take this as payment to help you get what you need from the Gene Spirit Hills."

"I'm still not sure whether I want to take you along, what is so important about that old piece of parchment anyway that makes you say that you will take it as payment?" said Father Todd,

"Well unless I am mistaken it did belong to the one-eyed witch conical she used to dabble in hells songs long ago, but was banished to the revolving lands set deep within hell itself. Oh go on let me keep it," Canting shouted. "Go on what are you going to do with it?" he added, smirking greedily.

"I…oh…go on then, keep it just as long as you keep to your word and help me get Tilde's flower," said Father Todd."

"You have my word as the word of a tree goblin," Canting replied. "My word indeed…" Canting held out his hand to accept the parchment with ease for he knew that this was a great gift and he would certainly gain from it in one way or the other…"Shall we be one our way then," said Father Todd, "as we have not got much time to get what I need."

"Yes hold on! I just need to gather up some tastiness for our little journey."

Hmm, Canting thought, what delights can I take…?

"Tastiness; I have some bits of food, you are welcome to eat with me," Father Todd exclaimed!

"Interrupting with haste of speed, err, I think not what passes my lips are clips of broken in two mud worms, dark bits of tree bark that have excrement's of slither beetles on. Crispy wispy leaves doused in slimy grimy puddle water and jackleg juice…you should try such an array of feed!" Canting laughed.

"Strange and deranged your choice there, I'll sub my little tub of stomach filling, thank you very much," muttered Father Todd.

"OK, that is your choice. You can't be licking your lips when I crunch and scrunch with my freckled, speckled tongue then!! have offered remember that, I shall go and collect what is needed. Give me a few moments then we can be on our merry berry way."

Canting hurried his little legs along climbed upwards over the tree which was his home opening, jumped downwards to the other side to gather. Seconds passed all of a sudden Canting was clambering back down his living branches.

That's me done I have everything I need now let's hasten with winds speed to souls greed.

That awaits us at Gene Spirit Hills.

Finally, rolling his eyes, Father Todd was thinking as the two of them strolled upon their way. Five minutes passed without a murmur from either of them.

Then, "Patchy catchy I am so scratchy my hands dance with contraband I live in my tree and will forever be a tree goblin. I rustle and bustle and in my song I prolong my fortunate, oh yes I do," nodding his head as he sung over and over! Father Todd was not impressed.

"A good song yes!! I like to sing; it brings happiness to my fore as I explore words," Canting looked up at the frowns which stared back from Father Todd.

"Yes, songs are good, however, I find it depends on what the song is about, how long have you been a tree goblin have you no family? Tell me more about you," said Father Todd.

"No I don't wish to talk about what I had and now have lost!" shouted Canting.

"Oh sorry I asked!"

"It's just, err, well it brings back certain things that I would rather forget."

"No, that's fine, forget it! I should not expect you to talk about things that you don't want to speak about, but I find that it is always good to share wisdom and one's life itself."

"Maybe later when we get to where we are going and we have eaten then just maybe we can express before we tackle and exhume the flower that you need," Canting replied back…as he broke out in song again:

"My name is Canting and always ranting on am I, I am one hundred and sixty three and I stand all two foot of me as a goblin of sovereign. I long to forever be remembered as the foremost tree inhabitant of these parts." Jigging and swinging his body and shaking his goblin body. Canting was happy as the two of them carried on their walk…

"So have you heard of the two Gauntlets of Balance then, Toddy?" Canting asked.

"Never, what are they? Sounds like something that you would put on a branch and carry on your shoulders," Father Todd cried out with laughter."

"Did you ever learn anything while you were learning the ways of your HEAVENLY book of text? Or did you just learn the art of stupidly frowned?" Canting said.

"Well, err, tell me then if you really have to thrust the information upon me there is no need to frown," said Father Todd.

"Uh you will have to let me ponder and gauge my thoughts, then I can explain in finer detail, why oh why my intelligence does tire my goblin brain sometimes. Let's take a rest for a while before my little legs start to peg with ache…"

Chapter 3

—✺—

"REST! A SMALL GOBLIN LIKE YOU SHOULD NOT HAVE TO REST!!! You should be like me, to be fit as a fiddle, as lean and bream as a stallion unicorn. That's how I am," derided Father Todd. "And that's how you should be…!"

"YES I should be," muttered Canting, "but as you can see I am a little wee tree goblin. And I must profess to your detest…Let's just forget about our little squabbles, rest in two, then commence our journey to capture and rapture your seek attained in the flower and all of its power…"

"I agree," spoke priest Todd, outlining his words with careful lips. "Let's do as you say. Let's commence in stepping over that broken twisted fence …For we will be and see what I seek very soon…"

"LET'S BE ON OUR WAY!"

"There is no perseverance on this the day of jitters…"

Among walking and talking they both were nearing Gene Spirit Hills, with a strange thrill that crept outwards between them both.

Rippling in mirrored like glistening mud! Yonder it stood before the two of them such a monstrous site at least four hundred feet and as wide girth as the heavens themselves and with a stench that would make any nostril want to curl up and hide under its fellow nostril. The kind of stench that makes sickness smell like a rose petal…

"SEE I TOLD YOU CANTING SPOKE. Still want to attempt the climbing?"

With a large frightful gulp, Father Todd gazed with open eyes…err! "Well I have no choice but to try…I have never seen such a scary sight but with my plight I must entrust my faith to leap frog any doubts that shallow creep into my mind…I need to think on a master plan and how I am going to span its berth!"

"They say that the easiest way is near the north side where the mud is at its hardest, but it's still as dangerous as a spawned shekel snake," spoke Canting. "There is one thing that could help you, it's a spell that I remember from a while ago that was used by ones that tried to conquer it."

"Oh?? What is that?" gasped Father Todd, "you are full of surprises, little one, but if it was used did it not do the ones that used it any good then?"

"Well I am not sure whether it would work now, but at least it may help you when you are half way up and you have to reach out and grasp the speaking branches that stick out of its mud…the spell is that of one called the Exceptional Chant of the Immovable Glove," answered Canting. "Once worn it has the ability to grip even the wettest and slimiest of things…but you are only allowed to use it once. And once only."

"And what are the words that have to be spoken replied Father Todd?"

"Well they are not much when the time comes for you to use the chant you must speak the words!

"Tisa Verna beta and elope ones traced and comb

Tombs of stone blasted trinkets

We settle at wallow beetle and borrow

In Ernst and mallow

Shake dips from unicorns tusk

Yet ivory settle on copper

The dragon's musk does ream?"

"Is that it," Father Todd asked, tersely. There is not a lot to speak in them words of a chant! Rather small in their context."

"Ah but it's not the content it's the words of true magic that make them work. Think of them as your favourite nursery rhyme that was read to you as a child," echoed Canting.

"HA HA," Father Todd cried out in laughter, and then whispered, "that's nothing like the nursery rhymes that were read to me. If anything I am a bit long in the tooth to remember such things…"

"Well at least try and remember the words," Canting mysteriously frowned.

"I WILL; let me give it a go, cattle mantle batter and wrangle," indulged Father Todd…

"HOLD ON! Wait just a minute, that's totally wrong!! Wrong, you silly man shouted Canting.

"Who are you calling stupid? I mean silly?" replied Father Todd, angrily.

"Well get it right then you must otherwise you may hamper and damper your chances of gripping them branches and getting to the top."

"Ok I will." A bemused Father Todd tried again and to the delight of Canting he somehow managed to get it right.

"YIPEE you got it," Canting jumped up and down."

Yippee, now all that's left to do is to put it into practice…" And it's like you have said that flower is so important,

Father Todd looked again at the mass of Gene Spirit Hills gulped then gulped again, he could feel the dryness against the back of his throat!! Then turned to Canting spoke quietly,

"Let's take our feet and beat them towards the north side and get it over and done with I am very afraid Canting!" jittered Father Todd.

"Well I don't expect you to be dancing to a demons jig, it's obvious that you will be afraid. How many unfortunate brave souls have perished within on trying? Listen, Toddy, what is of great importance to you? To try and retrieve Tilde's flower and banish them terrible dreams that you spoke off. And with them the nightmarish nightmares that drag themselves along in tow."

In reply Father Todd said nothing but from his looking you could tell that the wording of worried itself was now starting to descend upon his weary face...

SILENCE echoed itself around the open air space that surrounded the two of them. Finally they had reached the north side of the hills.

Father Todd lay down all his belongings against a medium double-bumped rock covered in bits of grass marshland, and with an untimely sigh turned to Canting and gave a kind of farewell glance and said, "Well, my little friend, it's time for me to go and tread upwards to reach this monstrous peak that stands before us."

"DON'T WORRY, just remember the chant and you will be OK, Toddy!"

Father Todd started the unbearable journey through a bit of marshland that he would have to walk through before his first steps were to step themselves from the bottom of the hills!

Turning back he glanced once more at Canting and raised a hand in a wave as his new friend became a distant object.

The look on the face of Father Todd by now had reached very grim and lost. But deep inside this had to be overcome!

Chapter 4

Father Todd had reached the bottom and was ready to take the first steps into the unknown but stopped with a look of surprise, in the near distance he could see a darkened cloud approaching!! his eyes were fixated as to what it could be, nearer and nearer it came, the thought of it being a cloud soon showed itself to be a hazy smoke, black and thickness was its outer and yet the inner looked clear except from a few colours that were mixed within it still fixated. Father Todd could not move his legs for they were non-movable…He wanted to shift them forwards well at least to move the rest of his body to get a more precise look. Again trying in vain he tried to have partial movement but however much he tried they lay static in their stance.

Closer and closer the smoke came and was now about ten feet away. Eight feet it was like Father Todd was now mesmerising its movement… six feet! four feet! Now it was almost within his arms' reach…

"WHO ARE YOU!!!!" a voice bellowed from inside the smoke. What do you want here? Why have you come to Gene Spirit Hills?"

Father Todd was now even more afraid than by the first thought of climbing up the hills! All of a sudden the smoke started to deteriorate and slowly vanish…

There in the midst of it Father Todd could make out a strange kind of figure shape.

At least eight foot in height, well so he thought! Within minutes of the smoke becoming smokeless his sense of clarity and vision became as clear as an eye's teardrop, or in an easier way of describing, as see-through as a glass fronted window.

Now the figure was there, there and real Father Todd gazed and gazed even more than before he could not see a face to understand whatever the being was! It had draped over it Some sort of mouton cotton garment that was heavily encrusted with rainbow embroidery stitching. Even the being's feet and hands were hidden.

Father Todd had no idea what to say or do he just stood in a lake-like frozen form.

"WHO ARE YOU," voiced once more from underneath the being's garment.

Plucking up the courage to speak, Father Todd replied, "Umm my name is Father Todd."

"AND WHY ARE YOU HERE?" threw the words from the being.

"Err...I have come to collect a flower from the top of these hills."

"ALLOWANCE IS NOT GRANTED."

"But you see I have to retrieve the flower, my travelling companion awaits me."

Within seconds of his outspoken words, Father Todd watched as the being removed its garment and to his amazement he could now see the being in all of its glory, with shock in shock he put his shaking hand over his mouth and stared as to what he was envisaging! There it was, the figure, the being; what surprised Father Todd was that she was a female. This mystical looking vampiress has slanted yellow eyes that lack both whites and pupils. She is bald. She is tall and has a narrow build. Her skin has an odd brown cast to it. Her feet have claw-like nails. Not that they could be known by Father Todd. She has wings that are more like shadows. She can turn into a whirlwind. She has mild telekinesis. Her diet consists of blood, but she can also eat normal food.

"Err, HELLO," came the words from Father Todd, nervously.

"I AM CASIMPRA AND I AM KNOWN AS THE GRANTER of wishes from the Unknown Pit of Wasted Wishes which is situated on the west side of these hills! I am also the watcher for Gene Spirit Hills. I have been for many years since it was decided by the new council of the kindred spirits of ennui!"

"Can I ask why I am not allowed up the hills, though?" asked Father Todd.

"WELL over a period of two hundred years one thousand and two hundred and fifty seven souls have perished here alone and it's something that the ennui hasn't stopped, you see there are rather evil forces at hand, and I knew that you would travel here in fact. I have presented myself before you for I alone understand your plight."

"You do?" muttered Father Todd.

"OH YES INDEED, you have the kind of nightmares that are so nightmarish, that's why you want to retrieve the flower and take it to the wise witch Tilde for you want a potion to curb of what I speak! I know more about you, Father Todd Amati, than you think, and more than you think about your little tree goblin friend, in fact you will become part of something great and you will help someone who will become famous in rich speak for centuries to come!"

"How can you know so much?" whispered Father Todd.

"That is something that only I can conceal and never discuss. I will mention one thing to you; I can save you the trouble of clambering up this hill. All that I ask in return is that once you reach shore's end you call into and speak with one shadow master that lives within the caves of thoughts, his name is Cerci, you must tell him that the twin warriors of stannic are no more, that they have now joined the Abdomens of

Heaven's Lure and will insure that the pact of promise will present itself when the time is ready. That's all you have to say!"

Father Todd agreed for if there was thing that he did not want was to endanger his life by journeying upon the hills and even more so after he had found out how many souls had perished…

"But hold on, how are you going to get the flower for me?"

"LOOK BEHIND YOU!" exclaimed CASIMPRA.

Father Todd turned around and to his amazement the flower lay on the ground. But how?

"It's like I explained to you, I cannot say, however, one day we will come before each other again! Pick up the flower and be on your way for your little goblin friend awaits your return…"

Overwhelmed and confused a little Father Todd leant forwards and with his long narrow fingers he reached down towards where the flower lay grasped it at its stem and picked it up…Holding it upwards he glanced at it in shock, a look of relief descended from his brow downwards over his chest and shadowed around his legs, the warmth of its feeling had made him aware how close he had actually become to within a whisker of putting his life in danger.

"Is that it can I go now? Am I right that all I have to do is to tell the one you named as Cerci?" he asked CASIMPRA…

"Yes you can go. Oh there is one thing, though," she spoke to him. "If you do not do as I have asked then the flower that you hold within your hand will lose its life of living and will become worthless to you…"

"I will make sure that the message you have asked will be relayed," Father Todd replied. Well then I will travel back to go and give my little companion the great news he will be very surprised as to what I have been granted by you…"

Chapter 5

Father Todd turned around and walked for a while and made his way back towards where he had left Canting sitting. His slow paces started to quicken as he was excited to tell Canting of his good news. Oh what a huge surprise it would be for his little friend…

A short distance had passed when Father Todd looked and could see Canting…

"Hey, Canting," he shouted over. "I am back…"

"Fantastic. Already? You have only been gone a little while, have you got it?" Oh, I was very worried indeed that you may have had trouble or that you would run into some difficulties."

"Quite the opposite you will never believe me when I tell you what happened and look what I have in my hand I have it I have the flower…"

Canting looked and smiled, "Oh yes, you have it," he replied. "It is a funny looking flower don't you think? But oh I am so glad that you have got it… But how? You don't have anything that tells me, you don't even look as if you have been up Gene Spirit Hills? Did you use the chant then?"

"Well," Father Todd said, "lets both go and rest over near the rocks and I will tell you what happened."

"Oh golly me, golly me… Canting hurried over to the rocks he was ready and waiting even before Father Todd had any whisper of chance to set off walking.

"Come on," he yelled back with smiling lips, "hurry up over here. Come on, Toddy; get your scrawny beanstalk legs over to these rocks."

"Hold on a minute, I am coming, I am just overjoyed by what has just prevailed…" said Father Todd as he reached the rocks and crouched down to rest his legs and socks boots.

Canting looked at him with a funny kind of oh well excuse me I am waiting to be told…

"Well? Tell me…"

"No," came the reply from the mouth of Father Todd.

"I'm wishing on a star," started to wander from Canting's lips.

"OK, you win," Father Todd threw back from his own lips. Canting waited in silence and started to listen to what had happened at Gene Spirit Hills.

Father Todd spoke of his nervousness and how much he did not want to travel up there.

WOW was the expressional look from Canting as he listened with open ears.

More and more he was told how from out of the nonexistence the flower was fetched forth to him and he explained what was asked in return of him.

An even bigger wow now expressed itself from Canting, he sat there with his little goblin jaw wide open.

"So there you go that's what happened while I was at Gene Spirit Hills. I am just so grateful."

"So am I," replied Canting. "It is wondrous what happened to you, wondrous indeed."

"At least now we can follow tallow to shore's end…"

"To be quite frank with you, Toddy, I was really worried, my friend, I was so worried that I may never see you again…"

"Was you? I was not aware that I had that sort of impact on you," glared Father Todd in slight amazement.

"But you do; I am glad that we had become travelling companions and the thought of losing you I just could not bear…"

"Anyway I am here and I am also OK," he replied to Canting.

"I think that we should now make our move towards shores end as we have to make sure that we don't lose or miss our travel…"

"Yes!!"

"Let's get a move on," Canting said as he stood up and outstretched his little arms…, "Our journey just gets better."

"It may not further down the line, you do realise that don't you. We have our sea trip yet. One that will be interesting, we have yet to travel through the Damned Tunnel of Mysteries," said Father Todd.

"Well I did not expect it to be as easy peaky," Canting said.

Father Todd stood up, yawned in tiredness and picked up his belongings, "Let's get jaggy then," he said to Canting.

Their four legs started their journey, once again they had been walking around an hour and a half, they had passed many plains of nature along their way.

"Can you hear the sound in the distance," Canting asked Father Todd.

"I hear what seems to be the sound of slavery waves I think maybe," Canting replied.

"That's exactly what it sounds like just above them smaller hills that stand in front of us."

The two of them carried on walking and reached the top of one of the smaller hills.

"Look over there in the water," Canting shouted.

To their surprise there it was in the distant front of them, the ship that would carry them on their journey!

"My it is such a big vessel," Canting looked at Father Todd with a worried look on his face. "Are you sure we should get on board?"

"Well yes we don't really have a choice do we?"

"Not really I suppose we don't," said Canting. The both of them walked across and down over the hills to the mangy sand, and made their way over to the left side of the shore to where the ship was anchored. Both of them could see the white waves of the ocean water crash and bash against its side.

They could also make out four figures standing around a burning fire on the sands in the latter distance. As they got closer they could hear, vaguely, a conversation taking place.

"Serene Captain, when set sail can I master at the ship's helm?"

"Oh we will see, I just maybe take a rest in me galleon bed, ahoy me crittles."

Canting and Father Todd looked at each other with frowned looks, what a weird some lot, they thought, as they both got closer they noticed one of the figures had noticed them.

He raised a hand and pointed towards them as he said the words, "Ah ha, newcomers to feast on," the other three turned around and looked straight at Father Todd and Canting.

"Oh hello," shouted over Father Todd. Shivers started to tangle themselves within his spine. "We have come to ask if we may travel aboard your ship."

"Oh you have?" one of the figures replied. "Come closer to us so we can see what may be our feast tonight."

Canting and Father Todd were now as close as they could possibly be and one of them who looked like the captain certainly looked as frightening as the character that was described to him…The other three figures were just as frightening.

"I am Inertia and I am the captain of *The Vile Jewel* and these are some of the ship's crew. Dragin! Elion, and Sebeth," both Father Todd and Canting were a little scared of what they had been introduced to.

Dragin This greedy male vampire has wide chalk-white eyes that never blink. His green hair is really a set of quills that he can use as a weapon. He is very short and has a lean build. His skin is white, but the blood flowing beneath it actually seems to glow. His feet have arrowhead-like nails. His joints seem to bend in ways that human joints don't. He can turn into a red mist that kills with one strike. He can control the minds of his minions. He has necromantic powers. If attacked with weapons made of any blessed material, he will be incapacitated. His diet requires blood of any kind. He feeds not through his mouth, but via mouths in his palms

Elion was not a vampire but a demon. This male demon has droopy grey eyes that seem to glow in the dark. His fine, straight, gold hair is worn in a style that reminds you of a strange headdress. He is short and has an elegant build. His brown skin is like a reptile's skin. He has a domed forehead. He can turn into a scorpion. He can be killed by destroying his heart. He feeds on psychic energy. Sebeth on the other hand was an angel who had joined the forces of evil and one that had become pure evil itself, a half angelic vampire who has almond-shaped orange eyes that are like two rising suns. His red hair is really a set of small snakes that he can use as a weapon. He has a broad-shouldered build. His skin has an odd blue cast to it. He has thin lips. He can turn into a cloud of dust. He produces terror with his presence. He doesn't suffer from standard vampirism disabilities. His diet requires blood of females. He feeds not through his mouth, but by his teeth that can stretch out from his skin.

Canting looked as scared as a fish in water just as it is devoured by an approaching pelican. Father Todd did not look much better in fact his moist skin seemed to have turned dry.

"Well, newcomers," said Captain Inertia, "and where do you want to travel to?"

"Er, well," said Father Todd. "To the three islands of justice."

"Well you can travel aboard within our ship."

"Oh yes!" the other three shouted, "we can feast together." Canting was now wondering would it be wise to travel.

"Me hearties, you will be safe," spoke out Inertia with a grunted out laughter. "How do you expect to pay for this journey?"

"Uh he has old parchments, some that detail magical words," spoke up Canting.

"Be quiet," Father Todd said.

"But you have."

Father Todd was not amused.

"Let me see," Sebeth shouted, "or shall I take them from you?" Father Todd handed all the rest of the parchments over.

"Here you go."

Captain Sebeth chucked the parchments over. Grasping them, Inertia examined them, his eyes lit up, particularly to one in question.

"Hmmm I could just take these," he said, looking at Father Todd.

"Err, yes you could," Father Todd murmured back.

"However, I will not take them, you can have the rest back I will keep this one," Inertia read the words that were inscribed on the parchment that he held in his hand.

"Creatures nail I have never death, fading beyond
any echo cry, your vixens have their cast:
in your most puff of smoke entrées are things which horsemen's shoe
me, or which I cannot dirt because they are too spading

Your spell look sacred will unmeant me though I have streams myself as be gone, you trickle fickle always begin by begin myself as in water (gales of winding cup of truth, gelding) her dwell out

Or if your in trail be to female unicorn me, I and my shout will battles very flutes of ret root, army of angels, as when the green of sheen of this echoer cry stones of talk the lost invisible imposable everywhere harmonising;

Nothing which we are to heaven above in this always hell below the help of your toads foot hath: whose scorch bells of non ringing me with the tally of its low, dawn breaking high and forest guardians with each the sign of 3ing

(I do not black what it is about you that blue and golden swords; only something in me clay the spirit of warriors of your vixens is spiders eye than all in) carve, not even the snow less winter, has such bats tail encased."

"And because you have given me this I will guarantee your safe journey, both of you!"

"What is it?" the Captain asked Dragin! Elion, and Sebeth, what does it say?"

"It will come in handy on our travels as you will see."

Canting and Father Todd were happy to hear the words that the Captain spoke, even if the both of them had doubts in their minds.

The fire that they were surrounding was now starting to drop its flames and the coldness of air from the sea waters was now starting to forth itself around them and was making the flames of red turn a yellowy purple.

"Ar ha bless me oh vagabonds, let's make our way to the ship."

Canting looked at Father Todd with a disillusioned look; there was no small boat that would ferry them to the ship how on earth were they meant to get across?

"Uh excuse me, how are we going to get to the ship?" Canting asked.

In reply Inertia shouted, "We will travel through the air." "Through the air?" said Canting.

"Oh yes, why would we take a small boat when we can travel this way?" Inertia said back to him as Dragin, Elion, and Sebeth, joined in the laughter of their captain.

"Toddy, can I have a word in your ear?" said Canting as the two of them gently eased their bodies firstly two foot then four foot then six and eight foot at least from the terror captain and his compatriots.

"What is it?" said Father Todd to Canting as he bent down.

"I am not sure about getting on that ship with them, how can we be sure we can trust them? And what is the feast that they are talking about?" Canting whispered in a low spoken voice.

"I'm sure it is their food that they will eat," replied Father Todd. I'm also sure that we will be OK, we have to take the captain at his word!"

"Well I won't be happy until we reach shore's end," said Canting.

"Ahoy our feastful travellers, we are ready to return back to the ship," Inertia screamed at them. "We have to go, we can't be a waiting for ya."

Canting and Todd made their way back to where these unbeastly souls were standing.

Then out of the blue Father Todd remembered that he had to go and see Cerci, something that Casimpra had asked!

"Canting he spoke...,"

"Yes, Toddy, "what is it?"

"I have to go and relay that message."

"What message...?"

"You know, the one that Casimpra told me to forward to Cerci."

"I remember but I had forgot," said Canting. "What are you going to do? You had better tell Inertia, but I'm not really sure, he will probably snarl at me."

"Tell him you must, Toddy."

"Umm excuse me, Inertia…"

"Arr, what is it?" Inertia bellowed back in nastiness of voice.

"Uhh, I forgot to say that I have to go and see someone!"

"Someone? What do you mean someone? There is no one around these parts for you to go and see, and if there was they would have already been feasted and breasted upon!"

"Captain let's not take them," snarled Sebeth, let me feast upon their flesh."

"BE QUIET!" there is no feasting going on here, well not yet," replied Inertia with a wicked tone. "Arr harr tell me about this someone who you want to visit. You could see the expression and look of Inertia was not a good one. TELL ME!"

"I have to go and give a message to the one who is known as the shadow master; he lives within the caves of thoughts which I am led to believe is somewhere around here. His name is Cerci," Father Todd said back, briefly.

"HE IS NO MORE!" said Inertia. He was killed in an onslaught one year past."

"He can't be. I have to give him a message," said Todd.

"You will not be giving any message. I have already said that he was killed."

Father Todd could not believe what he was hearing; it's impossible he thought; why would Casimpra tell him to give the message if he had been killed?

"I have no reason to speak of lies," shouted Inertia, "why do you need to see him?" he asked.

"Does not matter now," with a glum look upon his face Father Todd knew that the potion that was needed from Tilde was impossible to get.

"We should go," suggested Canting trying to cheer up Father Todd, "to the three islands, we have nothing to lose."

Thoughts entered Father Todd's head; how could this be? He could still not believe it.

"Come on snap out of it, Toddy." Canting knew he had to try and get his friend over the shock.

Inertia spoke, "We are going to the ship, we are ready to go; if you want to travel with us you had better make your way over here, the both of you, otherwise we will leave you behind. I will still keep this parchment though, haha," he laughed.

Crash bang the sounds of the white tipped waves smashed and banged against *The Vile Jewel* as Father Todd thought on whether he should chance his trip now. "OK, I've made my mind up," he spoke with Canting…

"You have made a wise choice there," Canting replied.

Err, well, so he thought, he was still not sure!!

"You both have to come over here," said Inertia, "and
stand in this circle we will all join hands."

I'm not holding any of their hands," Canting thought to 4 himself!

"Over here," Inertia said once more.

Father Todd walked over to join Inertia, Dragin, Elion, 7 and Sebeth, and stood within the ring that they had formed.

Canting, however, was still stood at least six feet away you 9 could tell that he did not really want to join them

Chapter 6

—⚊—

"Goblin, come here," said Inertia, or I will let Sebeth do what he wants with you...Come on, Father Todd," he demanded

Canting hesitated at first then joined them. He was standing next to Father Todd as he felt more at ease there...Father Todd reached down and grabbed his little goblin's hand.

"Give me your hand," Inertia said to Father Todd. Reaching out to grasp Inertia's hand Father Todd felt the ice of coldness that pressured against his own palm. Dragin grabbed Elion's hand, as Sebeth stretched out his long pointed brokentipped fingers to grasp Canting's hand. He gripped at the little goblin's hand firmly, looked at him with an awesome terror look and ran his tongue up against his upper lip and across his bottom lip then threw his long hairy tongue back into his mouth and laughed...

Brrr, that sent a shiver from Canting's head to his toes he was still curious with the fear of what was going to happen...

Inertia spoke, "Everyone must close their eyes and hold on tight while I say a few words to get us into flight..." they all closed their eyes and words started to echo from Inertia's voice box.

"Wind rain mist curls

Flight us to *The Vile Jewel*
Within clouds of swirls

All of a sudden as soon as Inertia spoke along appeared some grey mixed black smoke that swam in circles around them all.

Canting gave out a large shriek as he could feel his legs start to rise, Father Todd opened his eyes and spoke to Canting and looking downwards at the same time they were ten feet off the ground and still rising.

"Hey, open your eyes, Canting."

"No. No I can't, I am too afraid to open them.

A roar of laughter came from Inertia and the other three sending the echoes into the sky…Canting gently eased one eye open and peered downwards with a fright he quickly looked back up and closed his eye… twenty feet now they had rose but were heading in what was a straight line. Father Todd could see exactly what was going on but Canting had again closed his eyes.

"Yen rag err ha," Inertia shouted from the top of his throat.

Father Todd could now see *The Vile Jewel* with its dampness sweat that swells the air, as it became close with transparency nearer and nearer they got an eerie look and presence wallowed around the ship along with a smell of stale blood!

They were above the ship now.

"Let us descend and bend our legs," said Inertia." Their descent was taking place and still with his eyes fixed closely Canting just wanted to be on solid ground Well at least on the ship's deck. Within minutes they had landed aboard…

Canting could feel the hardness beneath his feet and opened his eyes.

"Are you OK?" asked Father Todd.

"Umm yes I am now," replied Canting,

The five of them let go of each other's hands and wiped bits of grudge sludge from their fingers onto their clothes he then looked around the ship's deck, it was long and vast, he could see the ship's wheel in front of him covered with a black liquid that was dripping downwards Canting's eyes were fixed on the ship's masts and sails they were as black as the darkest clouds that would follow the worst thunderstorm…each sail had skulls that draped from them with bits of lead beads attached. The ship stenched of the awful smell and its waft started to make its way up Canting's goblin nostrils; phew, he thought, reminds me of stale ale mixed with the tail of a cabbage worm rabid in its turning water… Canting noticed something shifting in the darkness near the far side of the ship.

Inertia shouted out to Canting and Father Todd.

"Welcome to *The Vile Jewel*, make this your home while we sail… crew of *The Vile Jewel*, show yourselves!"

The rest of the crew members must be down below Canting thought to himself. Hatches flew open on the left side of the ship, then to the right the rest of the crew started to clamber out. Canting sat down and perched his body onto the old cracken, creaking, crack o'jacked ship's deck and watched Father Todd, who by now was standing near four old barrels that barrelled toppled on one another…and watched…

One two three four five, at least twenty he could count, bones of figures or what looked like figures.

Then with a huge roar they shouted, "Our captain has returned!"

"Crew of *The Vile Jewel* we have two more crew members that will embark on the seas, make yourselves known to them…"

Strange, Canting thought, they were not like any of the others! Five skeletons paraded themselves to Father Todd and Canting; they had introduced themselves with a hint of a demonic smirk…they all spoke at the same time and it was made known that they were not skeletons as bones may be, they were in fact the five unicorns of Betrom, unicorns that had a magical sense about them. They had been cursed and cast in spell to be slaves of Inertia and the other three…Father Todd looked at

Canting as the crew scurried back below the ship's decking, clatter clink the sound their movement made… "Elion," shouted Inertia!

"Yes, my Captain."

"Set the masts for high tides as we set sail shortly." "Yes, Captain," he replied and roared!

"SEBETH!" Inertia shouted again. "Take our two travellers down below the ship and introduce them to our most prized capture…"

"Yes, Captain, I will."

"Come," Sebeth said to Father Todd and Canting, "get up.

Come along this way, follow me."

Father Todd and Canting both got to their feet and followed Sebeth to the open hatch not too far away from the ship's wheel…"Down there! Climb down," he instructed them. "Hurry up now."

Both of them climbed into the lower part of the ship …What is that stench they both thought, neither would dare to speak as they climbed below! They heard some echo words spoken by the most strange voice.

"Hey, Toddy, can you hear that?"

"Yes I can. I wonder who is speaking?"

You could almost sense the fear in both of their voices!

"QUIET!" snapped Sebeth as he followed them both below…Father Todd and Canting said nothing. They were listening to the words recited in full flow by a low husked tone voice.

All in the secret passage went my red daring
on a goats eye adventure of beignet into the bowl of stirring revolving
mirror.

boom crushed mushroom silver of guard end smoke and in the waned
nightfall before.

the ones be they than powers thirst the steeple stopple daybreak the stopple steeple waned nightfall.

boom inflicted reveal at a fire second century the earth vision before.

green become blue went my red daring darkening the speaking bush down into the bowl of stirring revolving mirror.

boom crushed mushroom silver of guard dew smoke and in the wind before.

water be they than purple mark the crushed mushroom fire nightfall the mist smoke n nightfall.

boom mist smoke at a beignets candle the magic poet the lost text before.

chime at invisible curse went my red daring darting the grey down into the bowl of stirring revolving mirror.

Blades' grass be they than golden decanter erotic the angels of time stars nightfall the crimsons' begonia nightfall.

boom the crests sign at the secret passage grey the be gone dies spirit before.

All in the secret passage went my red daring on a goats eye adventure of beignets into the bowl of stirring revolving mirror.

boom crushed mushroom silver of guard dew smoke and ink my bells letters chime before.

Chapter 7

Father Todd awoke with a slight crick in his neck, the wood pressing hard against his head. He lay there for a moment, feeling the sway of the boat before letting out a deep sigh.

"This is as safe and peaceful as it gets I suppose," Father Todd said with a slight groan in his voice.

"Indeed, danger comes to you, Father Todd, like an abundant weed." A little voice said with a sharp laugh.

Father Todd looked over at Canting, who was sitting on top of a shabby dresser. Canting was swaying with the ship, humming a slight tune to the waves as they heard each barrage the side of their cabin.

"Did they steal anything?" Father Todd asked, his mind still not fully awake to prevent his thoughts becoming words.

"Steal? Why would they steal from those that they can put to the steel? No, good sir, the crew of this ship has not one stealing cur," Canting said while his head made a slightly sickening bobble to the ship.

Father Todd heard his stomach growl as he turned his head away from Canting.

"Oh dear me, I'd hate to think what you can eat here for free." Canting frowned, scratching his stomach, "Although, the wood of this ship might make for a filling meal."

Father Todd yanked himself up and held the bedpost to gather his bearings. The sway of the ship increased exponentially as he tried to make a stand.

"You need to wait on your feet a little while before you have your sea-legs. If you don't wait, you'll get sea sick until the day you die." A gruff voice said as Father Todd held his mouth, feeling the vomit rise in his throat.

Father Todd looked up to see who had said it but there was no one at the door. However, he was too pre-occupied with making sure he could put food into a spout that only went one way. A plate slid towards him on the ground, it had a single pickle with an orange on the side.

Father Todd picked up the orange and began to peel away at it. The juice squirted on his fingers and seemed to relax his hands from aching, which threw him off slightly. He was not aware his hands ached.

As he ate the first few pieces of orange, Canting dropped down and looked out the door.

"Ooooh," he said with a slight awe in his voice, "I would do anything for that map."

"Is that so?" Said a voice that came from out of the corner. "It was a blessing from the sea demon herself. Would you still do anything for it?"

Canting jumped and ran to Father Todd's leg as Captain Inertia came inside the room laughing. He beckoned them both to follow him. Father Todd obeyed, hoping not to endanger his own life by refusing. He turned the door to see a room that had nothing but gridlines, lands, and dials everywhere. There was no floor, ceiling, or walls, just a large map that seemed to move on its own.

"The sea demon gave me this so I could stay on her ocean forever without ever getting lost. It's ruined a lot of the fun that being Captain was all about. Luckily, this map keeps my crew from deciding that it's best if I no longer reside as captain," Captain Inertia said with a smile. "It will disappear if I die for any reason and this thing is valuable. It's a complete map of whatever world we may be in."

"Where are we?" Father Todd bluntly asked.

"We are here." Captain Inertia pointed at what looked like a moving star on the map and then his finger travelled in a straight line to a group of islands. "This is where we are going."

"What a wonderful map and what's best is it doesn't look like a map," Canting said as he looked at it. "I have never left my land but I never thought the world would be this grand."

Captain Inertia bent down and picked the tree goblin up by his hair. "That is really annoying."

Canting quivered just above the ground, "I can stop but I can't say my speech won't…" he struggled not to continue talking but he burst out the last word with a gust of breath, "flop!"

Captain Inertia dropped the goblin on the ground and kicked him out of the room. Father Todd stood there, too stunned at the sudden violence. There was a resounding crash as Canting fell into the wood of the ship.

"Now that the annoyance is gone," Captain Inertia said with a smile, "Would you like to look at my map?"

Father Todd glanced nervously at where Canting had been before turning towards the map, "Where did we come from?"

"The Island of Misery," Inertia said, pointing to the land that was behind the ship, "Or that's what the rest of the world calls it after the werewolf massacres." "Massacres?" Father Todd asked.

"Normally, werewolves will just pick off a few people from random villages. Then in a giant surge, they captured the four shadow spirits in the current realms and ploughed through the island, which led to its renaming. A total of fifty million people lie dead and a further one billion have been turned." Father Todd gasped with shocked, "Oh my…"

"Yes, it turned quite a few eyes, which is why the angels and demons have begun fighting amongst themselves. The hierarchy of Heaven has unsanctioned a couple leagues of angels and the Demon realm is more than happy to deal in the tendrils of evil." Captain Inertia chuckled.

"You actually have that on the map?" Father Todd asked.

"Of course, Heaven's Gate is just passed the Academy of Magic, not too far from where we're headed. The Demon Spawn is in the complete different direction on the other hand." Captain Inertia shrugged, "I've never been allowed entry into the Academy of Magic though, so I doubt I'd be able to get entry into Heaven's Gate. I have seen it though, just a gate surrounded by water."

"Heaven is on Earth?" Father Todd asked with his jaw slightly hanging.

"As it is in Heaven, so too will it be on Earth. So why wouldn't the gates be here as well?" Inertia asked. "You priest folk always try to decipher the meanings behind the book but isn't there a passage that says you're not supposed to do that? There's a lot of things that conflict with what priests say and what they do."

"There's also a passage saying we should stop worrying about tomorrow but only the most peaceful priests can accomplish such a task. The Heavens understand though, they give forgiveness for when it's asked."

Captain Inertia looked at Father Todd for a while with a discerning eye before turning his attention to the map once again.

Meanwhile…

Canting landed against the wall at the end of that hallway, landing hard on the floor. He shook his head and stood up to on his root-ly legs.

"We must have that…for the cause…Dragin, will you…"

Canting heard these words travel into his ears in bits and pieces. When he looked over to the direction they were coming from, he saw a door slam shut in front of him. Canting went up to the door and leaned his ear against the wall while speaking in a mutter.

"Ear be not the one on my head, be the one on my space instead."

His ear grew into the wall and became whole again once it reached the other side of the wall.

"I do not like how convenient the only survivor on the island managed to find its way aboard this ship. Striking a deal with captain makes it even more suspicious."

"We need that flower. We had been trying to obtain it the entire time the captain landed on The Island of Misery's beach. How did food get a hold of it?"

Canting panicked, pulling his ear out of the wall and started to run towards the room where Father Todd was.

Canting burst into the room and hid behind the wall next to the doorway. Then he leaped his arms around Father Todd's legs.

"Canting?" Father Todd asked with a raised eyebrow.

"I heard the telling of fights and the ending of your sleeping nights," Canting stated with a whimper.

"What?"

Captain Inertia shook his head, "You carry something of extreme value, and they need to challenge me before they can kill you for it."

"That seems to be the consensus of the crew my... captain." A vicious voice travelled into the room.

"I figured it would be you Dragin. Have you allied yourself with the friends of your kingdom?" Captain Inertia said, crossing his arms as he looked at his vampire enemy.

The air between the two began to wane and Father Todd could feel immense pressure on his chest as the two vampires had a visual battle within the small place.

"Let us go to the deck," Captain Inertia said while gesturing his hand down the hallway.

Inertia followed Dragin up to the deck with the other two following shortly behind them. The entire crew seemed to have known what was happening because they had all gathered around in a circle on the ship.

Dragin stopped a few feet away before turning to Inertia who held his hands behind his back. A few seconds passed by and nothing seemed to happen but the crew seemed to be cheering at something as the two stood still. Father Todd watched for what seemed like minutes as the two stood staring at each other.

"Unbelievable, their captain is truly a frightening man," Canting said.

This threw Father Todd off as he looked down at Canting but what was even more bizarre was when he looked back up at the fight. It seemed as though the two vampires were caught and frozen in time as their fighting stances held firm on the deck.

Father Todd blinked once more and once again, they were in a different place. Father Todd began blinking as fast as he could and he began to see the fight, but no sooner had he begun to see the fight than it came to a crushing end. Captain Inertia slammed the face of Dragin into the deck of the ship and ripped off both of his arms.

In a shocking brutal way of death, Captain Inertia beat Dragin to death and crushed his skull in with the detached arms. Throwing the arms on the ground, he looked at his crew. "Anyone else want to challenge me?" He said with what he thought was a wicked smile.

To his surprise, the whole crew began to surge at him and one of them got close enough to stab him in the side, "Oh Crap!"

Captain Inertia grabbed Father Todd and Canting, moving them behind him as he backed them into the captain's lodge. The few crew remaining loyal to him fought their way to guard him from any more attacks. Father Todd ripped off his sleeve and pulled it apart as Captain Inertia fell to the ground, shortly after closing the door behind him.

"Hold still, I have to get this wound closed," Father Todd said in a hurry, "Canting, go find some rum."

"A drink you may need but your urge should stay without feed!" Canting yelled as he began looking for a place to hide.

"I need it for his wound," Father Todd said with a glare.

"He's a vampire." Canting's face went blank with confusion.

"Vampire wounds cut by other vampires heal similar to human wounds," Father Todd stated, "Vampires have numbing poisons in their nails so that their victims aren't able to use their brain waves to fight back. So when it touches vampire skin, the healing perk of being a vampire is greatly lowered."

Canting reach up from the rum off of the edge of the table and wobbled it over to Father Todd.

"This is going to hurt," Father Todd said, looking into Captain Inertia's eyes.

The captain nodded.

Father Todd poured the rum over the wound and quickly bound it as the captain howled in pain. No sooner had he finished the knot than Inertia grabbed the rum from him, quickly downing the bottle to ebb the pain.

"These cowardly bastards, I can't have an honourable duel with any of them," he said as he tossed the bottle at his desk.

The remaining driblets of rum flew onto the floor and Canting barely dodged the falling shards. Inertia struggled to his feet, keeping a hold of the cloth to make sure it didn't fall off. He stumbled his way to the cabinet and picked up a sword from inside.

He desperately threw the sword at Father Todd, who fumbled it and dropped it on the ground.

"They're coming."

A sudden explosion went off as the door imploded on itself next to Father Todd. Father Todd was sent to the ground with a loud "thunk" as his face hit the ground. The traitorous crew began to pile in on top of the remaining members and a few of them got through.

Father Todd unsheathed the sword and crawled backwards as the crew came in. The flames from the explosion began to set fire to the rum that lay on the floor. The traitors stood back as the flames came to a roaring height.

"There's a fire in here, get the water!" One of them said from outside.

The fire began to grow hot as Father Todd began coughing over the smoke that was engulfing his lungs. Captain Inertia grabbed the necking of Father Todd's shirt but his grip slipped, and he fell to the ground.

All Father Todd could think about was, *"I could have swum to the islands and would have been safer."*

The fire had covered the door at that time and Father Todd was beginning to feel weak from the lack of oxygen in the room. Inertia was making his way towards the windows in the back but he, too, fell prey to the lack of oxygen in the room. Meanwhile, the traitors continued to watch as the flames engulfed the room.

His delirious mind finally asked a most clueless question,

"Where did I put the flower?"

A torrent of air suddenly blasted into the room as one of the windows shattered and Father Todd felt the new oxygen enter his lungs. While the smoke was still choking him of most of the oxygen, he no longer felt as though he would pass out.

Looking over to where the window had been shattered, Todd saw that there was a new creature in the room. It looked like a small ball with vines growing out of it, standing on a single one of the vines while the rest moved freely in the air.

Suddenly, the vines grabbed the wood that was in flames and threw it out of the window to the ocean. Todd could barely keep up as he watched the creature completely put out the fire.

"Time for sleeping is not now; you have to treat the traitors to a good bow." It said as it smashed its vines into the onslaught of enemies.

"Canting?" Father Todd and Captain Inertia asked at the same time.

Todd could see some of the vines were on fire and he tried to put them out but to no avail. Canting whipped the flaming vines at the doorway to keep the enemies at bay, pushing further into the door so that the three of them could make their way out.

Inertia grabbed Todd and pulled him down into the left over hole from Canting's diggings. Canting followed quickly behind, closing the gap before landing on the floor of the ship back as the tree goblin Todd had known.

"I never knew a tree goblin could become a plant as a weapon." Todd said as they had a moment of silence.

Canting looked over his burn wounds, wincing at each touch before saying, "When one has an adverb in front, it usually means something quite blunt."

Canting attempted to get up but the burns on his body were too severe and he cried out in pain as he tried to stand up. Gingerly touching the wounds, he peeled off what looked like burn bark with goo attached behind it.

"A tree I was, but burnt seems to be my disabling cause," Canting said as he let out a heavy sigh.

Father Todd ripped off the other sleeve and placed the bits of cloth over Canting's wounds. Lifting the tree goblin up and on to his back, Todd looked around from Inertia who was lying on the ground, leaning against the wall.

"If we go out there like this, we'll be torn to shreds," Inertia said.

"What about the rest of your crew?" Todd asked.

"Most likely, dead or injured. The only ones I know are loyal to me are not from Demon Spawn. Most of those are from Heavens Gate's first district," Inertia said, "Farmers and people of little importance that needed to pay off debts too high to count." THUD.

THUD.

Crack!

Boom!

A huge ball of fur burst through the roof and landed on the ground between them.

"Captain, we need to get you off of this ship." It said.

'It' was beginning to stand up and 'It' was scary. Nearly eight feet tall with black fur covering most of the skin. Yellow eyes looking out from where Father Todd would normally expect but two more blood red eyes looking at them from its shoulders. Blue veins vined all of its body and its claws were longer than Todd's hands. It was so massive that it could barely fit into the hallway and it towered above them.

"Kentro?" Captain Inertia asked curiously.

"Yes Captain, we need to move you. They are opening a Demon Spawn gate," Kentro said.

Kentro was different from any creature that he had previously seen but there was one thing that Father Todd recognized that couldn't be altered. Kentro had a black snout instead of a nose just underneath his eyes. This creature was a werewolf.

Father Todd collapsed in fear as the painful memories surge into him, freezing him on the ground. He felt the claws pulling on his shirt as Kentro dragged him across the floor. Captain Inertia picked up Canting with his good arm and lurched forward.

"All I have to do to stop the gate is remove the line of dust but if the whole crew is powering it, the spawns will be relentless," Captain Inertia stated, "We need to get these two off of the ship if we're to have any chance of breaking the summoning circle."

Kentro nodded in agreement.

The two of them made their way through the hallway and up the ladder, into the main bay where the cannons were. The main bay was empty but the roar of the battle overhead made it difficult to hear anyone that was being quiet. Inertia peaked out of one of the cannon windows.

"We're almost to the island. If we can make it there, the witches will be able to guard themselves from the onslaught," Inertia said, looking back at Kentro.

"Sir, do we have enough time? They'll be down here any minute." Kentro replied, looking at his captain sceptically.

"We'll simply climb to the bird's peak and wait it out. Even if they were to take all of the routes, they would only be able to send three to four at a time. We can tunnel them." Inertia smiled.

Kentro grinned, "Absolutely brilliant, sir."

The group made their way to the middle of the main bay where the ladder for the bird's peak was located. Opening the door, Kentro headed up the ladder first, his shoulders barely squeezing themselves inside.

"I think I might pass out from lack of oxygen," Kentro bluntly stated as he struggled his way up the ladder with one hand.

"You'd better not or we're all dead. We only have a slim chance as it is." Captain Inertia let out a slight chuckle.

Kentro ignored the sarcastic comment and continued to make his way upwards. The noises from outside served as mile markers, growing faint as they climbed up towards the top of the ship. Finally, Kentro broke out the door on top and threw Father Todd onto the wooden deck of the bird's peak. He quickly jumped up and towered over Todd's useless body.

Peeking over the side, he could see a small army beginning to amass and his fellow mates struggling to stay alive as the number of enemies began to increase. The demons were spawning near the ship's wheel and they seemed to have managed to forget that they were all heading towards land. Kentro smiled at their ignorance.

Father Todd burst back into reality as his memories finally caught up with him.

"I forgot the flower in my room!" He said in a panic.

Captain Inertia and Kentro both whipped around, looking at him with a mixture of shock and anger. The one item that the traitors were after was nowhere near them.

"What do you mean it's in your room? That's the only reason why there's a freaking mini-war on my ship!" Captain Inertia yelled.

"Sir, I believe it is wise if you do not yell too loud. They might here you." Kentro pointed out.

Father Todd nervously laughed as he scratched his head, "I suppose I should go get it."

Captain Inertia frowned, "If you go down there, I'll need tweezers to get all of you off of my ship."

Kentro place his hand over the captain's chest, "Father Todd will need the experience."

Kentro looked into Inertia's eyes with a grave bearing and the two seem to have their own conversation before Inertia turned back to Father Todd, "Use one of the ropes to swing down. Keep your feet forward so you don't fall on your face when you land."

Father Todd grabbed one of the ropes on the bird's perch and looked nervously at the ground.

"Falling from this height will break a limb but it won't kill you," Kentro said.

Father Todd began to sweat with anticipation as he gathered up the courage to make the swing. Memories of his life flashed before his eyes as he looked downwards towards the deck of the ship.

Father Todd began to feel pressure on his back and, in a panic, he looked back to see Kentro was pushing him over the edge. He slowly fell through the air at first before the gravity forced him to pick up speed. The ground was rushing towards him when he began to feel the sweat of his hands begin to slip on the rope.

Faster than he could react, the rope reached its end and, in a whip like motion, Father Todd crashed through the deck to the cabin deck. Pain wracked his body as he looked behind himself to see a large gaping hole in the roof with varieties of demons surging through it. His skin crawled with goose bumps and he bolted towards the cabins to find his room.

Seeing the map room at the end of the hallway, he turned left into the room. There it was, sitting atop the dresser untouched and unharmed. Father Todd grabbed it with one hand and looked back out in the hallway. The demons had already made it down to his level and he needed to find another way out than the one he used on the way in.

Father Todd pulled out his book with his free hand and launched himself into the hallway. He heard the grunts of the demons as they saw him come into view. Bolting down the other corridor, he began to see that there was no way out of the cabin deck other than going down or going back.

Pulling up the hatch, Father Todd found himself in the cargo bay. He could hear the grunts of the demons growing closer as they ran after him down the hallway. Frantically looking for a way out, he saw the cargo-loading door at the far end.

By the time he had made it halfway to the door, the demons had made it into the room. Struggling to open the door, he had to set his book on a nearby crate to grab the whole handle to shove the door forward.

As it opened and the ship rocked from yet another explosion, Father Todd had a single thought as he hung from the fragile door.

"This could have been thought out better."

Father Todd stuck the flower in his pocket and swung forward on the door to grab his book. Narrowly missing a sword in his face that one of the demons swung, he glided backwards with the inertia of the door.

He begins to swing his book at the swords now trying to poke and prod him to death. His hand was growing wary of holding on so tight and his brain was too busy trying to keep him alive that he had no idea how to get out of the mess.

The demon fell through the open doorway and into the water below as it swung again but with too much force. This made Father Todd happy and it gave him a few seconds to look around.

"I can climb up!" Father Todd thought, looking up at the straight line to the top of the deck.

Father Todd began to yank himself upward, putting his book in between his teeth so that he could use both hands.

No sooner than he began to climb up did he see something out of the corner of his eye. He took a moment to look at what it was, squinting at first but then he realized it was someone swinging on a rope towards him. Father Todd began to climb faster, hoping to avoid being gutted on the side of the ship but he was too late as he felt the pain hit his side.

His eyes closed and he expected to feel liquid but as he opened his eyes, he saw that an arm was carrying him. Father Todd looked up to see Captain Inertia looking straight ahead, as they turned the bow of the ship and made their way to the main deck. In a weird way, Father Todd felt his heart flutter and he found his next thought odd.

"God forgive me for I have sinned…wait, how have I sinned?"

He was not given the time to answer his own question as they landed abruptly on the deck. Captain Inertia grabbed Father Todd's necking to prevent him from falling on his face while swinging away with his sword. In a flash and flurry of movements, Captain Inertia was blocking every enemy around them but Father Todd still felt as though his body was being pressed in upon by the enormous crowd that surrounded them.

"How are you doing this? I thought you were injured?" Father Todd asked.

"I was but I have a werewolf on my ship. My healing power may have been slowed but there werewolf blood isn't affected the same way," Captain Inertia said with a smile, "The first mate was the only one who stood a chance."

Father Todd heard a crash as he saw a black object crash into the deck of the ship. When he turned his head, Kentro was holding out Canting for him to take. Father Todd nodded and gingerly grabbed the wounded tree goblin, sitting between the two monstrosities of the ship. That's when it began to rain blood as the two furiously fought off the demon spawn army.

The island was now well within view and it would only take a few minutes for them to reach the shore. Father Todd felt a hand grab his arm and Kentro turned his body to cover Captain Inertia.

"We need to get back up to the bird's peak. There's simply too many." Captain Inertia yelled over the roars, clashing metal, and drowning sounds of explosions going off nearly everywhere on the ship, "We'll need a running start and you need to hold on to me tight or you're going in the ocean."

Captain Inertia helped Father Todd to his feet, his face now covered in blood and his back bending over to protect Canting from any possible damage. Kentro got in front of them and all of them began to run to the side of the ship as Kentro tossed demons aside with his sheer size.

In a leap of faith, Father Todd tightly gripped Inertia's neck with one arm and held Canting in the other as they swung off the side of the ship. In a quick motion of swing, they climbed into the sky where Captain Inertia peeled Father Todd's hand off to let him fall into the bird's peak as they passed by.

Landing with a sickening crack, Father Todd cried out in pain as he looked down. His hand was a throbbing purple and Canting was lying unconscious on the hard wood of the bird's peak. Glancing over the side, he saw Captain Inertia and Kentro fighting fiercely on the ropes. Their bodies swung in close to the deck, picking off what they could but the spawning forces began to grow so much that there was no more room for them on the ship. Many of the demons were simply being tossed off the side of the ship.

Father Todd leaned in against the wall and cradled his hand, which wasn't moving. There was an odd peace to the moment, as the sounds of battle seemed to take place a half a mile below them. Looking into the sky at the glaring sun, which beat heat and warmth down upon them, Father Todd felt a strange sense of silence.

There was something there though and, as he looked further into the sky, Father Todd had a growing feeling that they were being watched. Then he blinked and whatever it was had disappeared but the strange feeling of being watched continued to linger.

"Brace for impact lads! Land Ho!" Someone called out below.

Father Todd crawled over to where Canting lay on the wood and used his body as cover for the tree goblin, pressing down with his chest so he didn't move. In a sudden shaking blast, his body was thrown from side to side as the ship collided with the land.

His hand throbbed with pain and in one sudden motion; he felt the ground leave his body. Floating in the air, Todd saw Canting coming with him. He reached out with his broken hand and pulled the tree goblin into his chest, holding him tight.

The ground came up to them fast as they came crashing down. Father Todd tried to cry out as he felt his body be crushed by the impact but his lungs seemed to have failed him, possibly because they were broken. His brain had become familiar with being on the verge of passing out by now.

He lay there, looking out at the ship that he had been on and felt a liquid climbing down his head. For some reason he felt the warmth of the liquid and it was starting to make him tired.

"I'm going to die... I'm going to die here..." He thought despairingly.

Captain Inertia and Kentro were running towards them before Father Todd's eyelids began to close.

"Maybe it's not so bad...I did come here to get rid of my nightmare... not what I expected though..." His last thoughts said as he slipped into the world of darkness.

The battle raged on as Father Todd slept and two beings came running towards them.

"Lily, alert all of the witches and tell them we have the flower!" Captain Inertia said, "They opened a spawn gate on my ship."

Lily Trotter stood there amongst the commotion in her long trench coat. Lily was rather tall for a woman but the black trench coat that she wore was still longer than her body. Her hair went down her back as it swayed in the wind, shadowing over her glasses and hiding a good portion of the pale white skin on her neck. Atop her hair was an old hat that shadowed her face completely but the most notable portion of her body was the black wings on her back and the bright red horns wickedly poking her hate upwards.

"Come wind, come air, aid my voice so that all can hear!" Lily said as she cast her spell.

All witches to the beach, there are intruders.

Suddenly the rest of the island was in an uproar as the witches came out of the cottages, their robes swishing behind them as they hovered themselves towards the beach. In an array of individual wands, every witch began to cast their spell as their wands pointed towards the beach.

"Air and water, hear our cry, let all who are enemy pass this barrier to die!"

A large watery barrier surged out of the ocean and strapped itself to their wands, connecting together with the other wands to make an island wall of the barrier. A few of the demons who had managed to make it on to the island charge the witches but as soon as they touched the barrier, their bodies disintegrated before reaching the other side.

Captain Inertia dropped down in front of Father Todd and looked up at Lily Trotter. He didn't say anything but he also didn't need to say anything.

"He'll make it." A kind voice said as he felt a hand touch his back, "For a vampire, you have a good heart."

Captain Inertia began to rummage throughout his body, finding the flower underneath his second shirt and covered in blood. Pulling it out, it unfurled and bloomed perfectly as if it had not been within Father Todd's clothing.

He handed the flower to the witch before turning back towards the battle, which was increasingly growing on the shore.

"You best fix the ship's heart." The witch said.

The witch was different than most of the witches in area, one eye that seemed to penetrate your soul and wrinkles with no end in sight. She could be considered a dwarf by how low she bent over and she wore a flower dress instead of a witch's cloak.

She struggled down with her cane and looked at Father Todd. Shaking her head, she cleared her throat and, with the softest voice he had ever heard, she began to sing. Hand on his chest and the flower in front of her mouth, the words began to flow.

Oh sweet sweet son of mine
Where have you gone
The blood I gave you
Now leaks toward the dawn
Let this flower heal
What the tears cannot
For with you gone my son
My heart all a knot
May your bones be one

Let your blood come back
Oh my dear son
Hear my words and come on back

Captain Inertia heard her words and turned his head with an eyebrow raised, but his curious thought would have to wait for later. He bolted back through the barrier and ran towards his ship with sword in hand. Kentro had been busy making sure that no new spawn came out of the gate but Captain Inertia saw his first mate closing in on him quite fast.

Captain Inertia bit his thumb and used the blood to smear his legs, "Speed, speed, give me more bloody speed."

It wasn't much of a spell but it did the trick for Captain Inertia most of the time, his blood poured out of his thumb and onto his legs in a solid line. It fuelled into his legs and his muscles grew ripe with tension as they increased in strength. What would have taken a few minutes only took a few seconds and Captain Inertia collided into the side of his first mate, sending him sprawling into the ground.

He leapt on to the demon and tried to plunge his sword into him but it was caught by the demon's gauntlet.

"You will die stubborn bastard!" Captain Inertia yelled as he bared his teeth and bit into the demon's neck to finish him off.

Dragin grasped at his throat and clung to it, trying to stop it from bleeding but they both knew that it would only be inevitable that he would die there.

"Why Dragin?! Why would you betray me?" Captain Inertia screamed at his first mate.

Dragin began to shed tears as he looked at his friend. It was rare that demons would cry because blood would come out of their eyes.

"We all have a first loyalty." Dragin said in a battered breath, "Mine was too old to get past."

Captain Inertia wrapped his arms around the demon, holding him tight with his tears pouring out of his face. Rocking back and forth, his body shaking with grief.

"I had to…you made me…you know you did…" He muttered underneath his tears.

Dragin reached up with his free hand and patted Inertia's back, "I know. It's okay, this was what I wanted."

There was no silence around them but as the two of them held each other, they could not hear anything but their own voices.

"Captain…" Dragin began.

Inertia pulled back and looked at his friend, "Yes?"

Dragin smiled, "The tree goblin is hiding something."

Inertia sat there in shock, "What? What is he hiding?"

Dragin began to open his mouth but Inertia could see the life from his eyes leave him before any words could make it out. He held the dead body of his friend close to him and cried out in agonized grief. A few minutes passed by before Captain Inertia got up and looked at the mess that was his ship, with the demons nearly everywhere and most of his crew barely able to fight.

Reaching in his pocket, Captain Inertia pulled out a key and looked at it carefully before nodding in agreement with himself. He pushed the key into his chest and turned it.

"You will pay for what you have done."

Lily Trotter looked at the scene and pulled out a toothpick from her pocket. Her thoughts began to twist and turn as she watched the battle before her unfold. She pulled out a notebook and began to write in it with magic that flowed from her finger.

Demons are bound by something from where they live, even if they choose to go to the other side. This was not in the library. I have located my father it seems, according to the pictures from my case file. Orders?

There was a slight pause before a reply began writing itself on the notepad.

How did you find out this information?

Her mouth made a tick in irritation.

Watching C.I. Inertia communicate over the death of his friend, his first mate. From the lip sync, the only reason why he turned on his friend was from quote on quote, "We all have a first loyalty."

She saw the reply come back hastily.

Apprehend father for questioning. Do not engage in the battle unless necessary.

Lily Trotter looked at the piece of paper with a disgusted look on her face but she chose not to reply. As she closed the book, a few words were scrawled on the leather cover.

Valley of Death

She always found it amusing that this is what they called it but she never truly knew why. Lily sat on the ground and continued to watch the carnage before her. She had gotten used watching carnage from the side-lines because she was just there to watch most of the time.

Captain Inertia was a good confidential informant for issues that happened in the Demon world and she was worried as to whether or not his cover was blown. Crying over a demon instilled many things into the surrounding people.

The crew that had turn traitor had eyes that reflected remorse for what they had done and pain for not being able to fix it. At that moment, her book began to vibrate in her hand.

She opened it to see a message waiting for her.

Dragin is referring to a summoning.

Lily let out a sigh. A summoning meant a lead and a lead meant answers. Out of the corner of her eye, she saw a few of the crew go below deck.

"Hmm, what are they up to?" she asked aloud.

Lily turned to the beach side that wasn't covered by a barrier and looked into the water. She crouched down beside the water and spun her finger inside of it. The water began still and she began to see the few that had gone below deck. They were writing inside of a book and all of them waited for something to happen. Then they all nodded and headed back on deck.

There's another book in that ship. She wrote.

Running interference, will relay the connection.

She waited for a bit, looking down into the water, knowing she was going to have to get that book. Sure enough, the message came back to her.

Obtain that book.

Meanwhile

Captain Inertia had used the key on his immortal heart. The trade-off began to show itself as his body began to grow in presence. He began to charge at the spawn gate and with each step that he took, he sent demons flying away from him.

At the spawn gate, Kentro waited for him and the two of them began to shove the demons back into their gate. Enormous blasts of energy shot out as Captain Inertia did his best to shove the demons back inside long enough for him to break the summoning circle.

"I've got this, destroy the gate!" Kentro yelled to him over the sounds of the demons roars.

Inertia bent down and looked for the summoning circle but it wasn't there. Nowhere would it have normally been if done correctly.

"It's not here!" He yelled.

Kentro scrunched his brow as he buried the demons in their gate, "It has to be below deck."

"There's no summoning circle that doesn't call its gate elsewhere. That's the point of the gate." He yelled back.

"There has to be! That's the only explanation."

Captain Inertia got up and ran to one of the holes in the deck of his ship. Dropping down to the next level, all seemed quite and he hurried to where he thought the circle would be. Underneath the circle and the deck, he looked carefully to see if he could find it. It could have been smaller than his nail with the level of skill on this ship; they had always been good users of magic.

There was no summoning circle at first but then he realized something strange. The wood of that area was new and he reached up to scratch off some of it. His nail caught a piece of wood and it chipped off. Underneath it was a pulsing vein and Captain Inertia's mouth dropped in shock.

He felt himself being yanked up as Kentro's hand came crashing through the roof. Captain Inertia landed on his feet and began helping Kentro out with the demons.

"It's Demon Spawn Bark," he said.

Kentro was caught off guard for a moment and a moment of silence passed between the two.

"I'll need to go see the witches," Captain Inertia said.

"There's no time, we'll have to rip the boards out." Kentro stated, "The wood can only summon if there's enough blood to run it."

Captain Inertia bent down to try and pry it loose but it would not budge. He placed his butt on the ground, meditating and concentrating on the magic. Around him, a spiralling cloud of black began to grow. He was unaware that it was flowing out of his body but Kentro had to move away from him. Kentro was worried about the captain for only a moment when he saw a demon try to strike him but the hand that was going downwards disappeared at first. Then the demon was sucked into the black cloud and Kentro only heard the screams as the demon died inside.

Suddenly, the boards underneath the portal began to crack and splinter as the cloud seeped its way inside. The battlefield on the ship was growing more intense and Kentro saw something bound its way towards them. In a red cloud, something was charging its way towards the ship and Kentro could smell something strange coming.

At the Cargo Bay

Lily climbed inside as the door swung shut behind her. As expected, it was musty and dirty inside. The only thing Lily always hated about pirates was their unusual ability to stay nasty. There was actually quite a bit in this one that didn't involve some type of riches in some way, which seemed odd to Lily considering Captain Inertia was an infamous pirate.

She made her way through the random bits of luggage and went up the stairs into the cabin deck. Lily braced the wall as she saw Captain Inertia jumped down in front of her but ignore her completely. He was most likely trying to close the portal to save everyone and his ship.

Turning into a room, she began to shovel through the drawers, trying to find the book. A crash came from another room but her brain simply ignored it. Sure enough, on the third drawer down the book lay their among some clothes.

Picking up the book, she peered inside. She groaned and closed the book, kicking the dresser in frustration. Lily plopped out her book again.

Transmissions are in a foreign language.

Write some of it.

She opened the book back up and began to write in her book a copy of what was written.

Az áldozat már megállapította.

A few minutes went by before she got a reply.

It's Hungarian, most likely werewolves. Keep the book so we can trace its location, there is someone who sold their book. Extract immediately and find a safe place for pick up.

Lily shook her head.

Apprehension of my father?

That can wait, books are more fragile.

Father Todd?

Extraction as well.

She reread the words scrawled on the inside of the paper.

Human… extraction? Confirmation please.

Confirmation not granted. This is of the highest authority, extract Father Todd and the book immediately. Father Todd is not human.

Her face made a random selection of weird faces trying to comprehend what was being said.

Father Todd is no human. Confirmation please.

*Father Todd is **not** human.*

Lily Trotter tipped her hat in silence as she put both of the books in her pocket. She knew that the message she got would go unanswered until she got Father Todd to Heaven's Gate. Lily would have to wait until they were in the safe zone before these answers would come out.

She went back to the back of the ship and dropped out of the cargo bay door on to the water. Lily walked on water back to the shore and headed towards Father Todd. She would have to wait until the ship was repaired before they could all head to Heaven's Gate, Father Todd would need permission to get into Heaven's Gate before they could go there.

The red cloud came up on them fast as Kentro did his best to cover the captain. The heads began to make their way out of the crowd just before the uncanny roar followed shortly behind it.

The creature was covered in a blazing fire and it had five heads, all in the shapes of dogs. Even though it looked like it had shape, there was no fur or anything to distinguish it from a shadow. It spread its way to the deck of the ship and the cries of demons could be heard as it ripped through them like they were bits of tree.

Kentro looked down at the captain, who was desperately trying to remove the wood but it was only coming inches at a time. Spuds of energy flew off with the removal of every piece and it may have refused entry to many demons but it was far from unstable.

The Cerberus made short work of the demons in front of it and quickly found its way to Kentro, who howled a greeting at the creature. It stared at him for a second and then snouted its disapproval before turning towards the rest of the demons.

Kentro actually felt the lack of surging demons become more prominent as he hesitated in between moments where there was no one to fight. While the portal was still shooting out demons, it wasn't shooting out very many anymore and the demons that were already on the ship seemed to have greatly decreased in numbers.

Kentro looked down at his captain, who was now starting to sweat on the outside of his body. His skin had begun to lose any colour that it'd had as he continuously focused his magic on the boards. Nearly half of the wood had been broken off and now there were no demons coming through the portal. Kentro didn't even need to fight because Cerberus was hunting down the remaining enemies, which made Kentro snicker as he remembered the beast's disapproval of him.

He caught a glimpse of a woman coming in from the beach and the hair on his skin stood up but he had no idea why.

Father Todd painfully awoke as the consistent roar of the magic barrier blasted his ears. Blinking, the ship began to come into focus and he felt relieved to see most of the people he knew were still alive. His body didn't have enough strength to turn so he rolled his head to his other side to look at Canting.

The tree goblin was still covered in his makeshift bandages but Father Todd smiled as his chest rose and lowered, showing that he was breathing. For such a small creature, he had sure shown his bravery in the midst of battle. As he thought about it, so had he with the charging into the ship and fending attackers off with a book. When he remembered the book, he tried to laugh but ended up coughing.

A sudden blast of explosive energy was sent out over the island as the portal finally collapsed in on itself. Captain Inertia and Kentro were tossed backwards, with Captain Inertia collapsing on the ground from exhaustion. Cerberus was the only one who remained unaffected as the few enemies left standing were wiped out since their connection to the portal was gone.

Kentro lay there, looking up at the sky and finally enjoyed the long awaited peace after the battle. The witches stopped their barrier spell and went back to their village. Only the oneeyed witch stayed behind to look over everything and Father Todd lay weak on the ground along with Canting.

Now that there was no more noise, Father Todd began to appreciate the simple things on the island. The smell of the ocean breeze coming in without the constant tossing of the ship was one of them. The sun was in just the right position to let a cool breeze of the ocean air to come in and it soothed everyone's pains as they all took a long breather from the battle.

Kentro tried to sit up but now that the adrenaline left his body, he began to feel his body return to normal. His long brown hair came back into place of his bronze-like muscle. His snout disappeared to make way for the stubble chin and button-like nose. He sighed as the rest of his body turned back into human form, he had mixed feelings about having to give up this amount of power.

Lily Trotter came into view as the dust cleared. She first went into the area where the spawn portal had been. Opening her notebook, she began to write inside.

Demonic bark made its way aboard C.I. Inertia's ship.
We have no way of back tracking this.
It happened between the time of departure and arrival.
C.I. departure… is not in records Why is it not in records?
We will find out.

Lily didn't like this; demonic bark was only found in the heart of Demon Spawn. Only demon hierarchy had access to it and it somehow made itself a part of Captain Inertia's ship while he wasn't looking. The possibility of that happening without someone noticing from Heaven's Gate is difficult to comprehend.

She frowned as she looked over the parts of what was once alive. Lily could have used recall magic to reverse its steps or previous magic to glance images it remembered. Now, those spells would be useless.

"Hmm, stupid gums."

Spitting out the toothpick in her mouth, she placed her hand over the bark. Lily began to feel the dread that seemed to leak from the bark.

"Where have you been?" she asked the bark.

She picked it up to smell it and then lick it. The taste was more than she expected, bits of hoof caught in her mouth and she had to spit it out. The smell was similar to what could be smelt by the sea.

"Minotaur?"

Lily walked over to Captain Inertia who was lying unconscious on the ground and placed her hand on top of his head.

"Spend the time, make your memories mine," she said.

An image of warming the hands by a fire.

An Octilius attacking the ship.

Watching the moon while sipping on a glass of wine.

A Minotaur waving as the hand waves back.

"There you are. Memories of mine become clearer than time."

Day 18 of June

Captain Inertia was writing in his logbook as the morning arrived outside of his window.

It seems we will be at the Island of Misery shortly after our departure here. It is always a pleasure to stay in Minotaur country because they make such good wood. Their wood has held this ship together for many years. —Morning log

Captain Inertia sighed as he looked out of his window. The Land of Gallopers was named rightly so as the wild horses charged their way past the ship below and the Minotaur village was nothing more than lumber houses. There wasn't a single bit of concrete or plushy gel substances anywhere; it was all natural with no magic. Something that Captain Inertia had come to appreciate.

He got up from his chair to go look at the repair work being done on the deck. The old wooden planks that had been damaged were being removed with the new lumber boards sitting beside his crew. A Minotaur stood there to watch the work and to help out where needed.

"Where do you find such good wood? Ever since I came here long time ago, I can't find any better wood," Captain Inertia said with a smile.

The Minotaur laughed, "Of course not, we have a special recipe for our wood. It took me a while to get this wood but it's rather…"

Lily didn't bother to wait for the memory to finish. She repeated the spell to read the Minotaur's memory of where the wood had come from.

A large catch of fish.
Captain Inertia landing on the island.
Chopping the wood.
Walking into the forest to get some wood.
Lily made that memory clearer to focus on it.

"Well ol' ax, I wonder what type of wood we'll get today. Maybe some redwood would be well for the collection. Captain Inertia has a habit of needing wood every month and redwood is the strongest on this land… maybe it'll last longer." The Minotaur said with a hearty laugh.

He began walking in the woods and examining the different trees, knocking on the side to see how thick they had become. After travelling for a little while, he began to hear what sounded like a heartbeat. Following it, he slowly began to find himself in the darker part of the forest. It stood tall with the wood itself seemingly pounding like it had veins.

The Minotaur looked at the tree and laughed, "A living tree, haven't seen one of these beasts in a while. It'll be just what the dentist ordered for that vamp's sweet tooth."

With a great swing, he began to chip away at the living tree.

Breaking out of her trance, her book had begun to vibrate within her hand. She opened it up.

Olodun sold the seed to the Minotaur.
How did Olodun even get a devil tree seed?
Olodun has no memory of doing it.
How did you know it was a Minotaur?
We backtracked through Olodun's memories.
I came to the same conclusion but from a different perspective. C.I. Inertia is fine, cover is fine but all leads he had with fellow demon spawn lay dead around me.
Confirmed. Bring C.I. Inertia in for debriefing; we believe he can be useful with this investigation. There's been activity at the Harbour of Horrors.
Father Todd has the flower undamaged.
Really?

Lily laughed at the reply. All the angels thought he'd die and it was miraculous that an enemy would just give it to him.

Yes, he obtained it through unusual means.
Leave the flower with Dame Castropal. She will be able to use it for quite a many things if the flower doesn't die on her.
How is Dame Castropal going to prepare spells, isn't she a dead witch?
She is a shadow ghost in the making.
You can make a shadow ghost?
Confidential.

Lily saw the reply and threw the book against the wall,

"Useless Angels!"

Lily came over to Kentro and looked down at him, which made him look up at her in return.

"Dad," Lily said blandly.

"Daughter," Kentro said with a snort.

"How ya been?" Lily said with a smile peeking out of the side of her mouth.

"Furry," Kentro said with a smile.

Lily chuckled, "Never gets old really. How's pirate life treating you?"

"It's difficult but worth it. Better than what my family is doing, excluding you."

"Okay, well, I'm going to drag you and Inertia into the camp fire area." She stated.

Lily grabbed the hands of her father and the good captain, and began pulling them towards the cottages. The most work was the beach, where the sand blocked most of her way. Once she got to the grass, it was much easier to drag them along.

Her father was lighter than she expected and it was a relief that he wasn't injured. Lily didn't sit well with family injuries and her temper tended to get the better of her. Inertia wasn't really hurt at all but he did need a more comfortable place than the wood of his ship to sleep.

In the middle of the cottages, there were two things; the town cauldron, because it was a witch village, and a well-made fireplace. The sun was beginning to go down and many of the witches had begun to come out to light the fires for the night. It would provide many of the crew with warmth but it was mainly to cook the witch's food once it had been summoned.

Getting food on this island required magic of an unusual kind, which was why most of the witches were here in the first place. You can summon animals but you still need to kill them, skin them, and cook them. Making a fire by yourself and keeping it in your house was dangerous, especially when you had valuable potions everywhere. Many magic cities showed similar aspects, as a way to prevent the ebb of time on their magical parchments and easily spoiled stores of potions.

Lily let go of her father at the campfire and followed the one-eyed witch into her house with Captain Inertia trailing behind her. He grunted as his body parts hit some of the furniture inside and Lily found herself being watched by Father Todd. To her, he was an odd man and she was rather sceptical about whether he could normally survive the same battle twice.

She lifted Captain Inertia off of the ground and slumped him into the bed, where he hit his head on the head rest. A loud grunt came from his mouth and he made a half-grab towards the pain. Then he quickly fell back asleep.

Lily rummaged around for his key, finding it buried in his back pocket. She slid it into the vampire's keyhole and turned it until she heard a locking sound. At the same time that the lock clicked, he woke up in a panic. Lily placed her hand on his chest, easing him back to the sheets.

"You fell unconscious." She stated.

"Is everyone safe?" Captain Inertia asked.

"Yes, everyone is safe and the battle was won."

Captain Inertia pulled himself up, "I need to get repairs done on the ship to make sure it's ready for sailing."

Lily sighed in slight frustration as he walked out of the cottage, "After I had the trouble of carrying you in here. Stubborn bastard."

"To think I was scared of him when I first got on his ship," Father Todd said with a nervous laugh, trying to start up a conversation.

"Hey Captain, wait a moment," Lily said.

Father Todd watched as she ran out the door.

Captain Inertia stopped to let her catch up.

"I have a few questions for you," Lily stated.

"I may have answers for you," Captain Inertia said snidely.

"Who is the Minotaur you buy your wood from?" Lily asked.

Captain Inertia waited a moment before replying, spreading his hands out to the sun sarcastically, "The... wait for it...Minotaur!"

Lily snatched him by the cuff of his shirt and got close to his face, "Listen, vamp, don't make me get nasty. You wanna see me get nasty... again?"

He shook his head, "I don't know his name."

"You've been going to him for years and you don't know his name?"

"Look, I go there for wood, not to settle down. I don't bother to remember the names of creatures I don't expect to see alive again," he said as he peeled off her hand, "I did as you asked, brought you that stupid flower, and lost my friend for your cause."

He leaned in close to her, "Respect."

Lily leaned in closer, "You bought demon wood."

His eyes grew wide with shock, "I did not."

"I looked through your memories. The last time you repaired your ship, the merchant sold you demon wood," Lily stated.

"He said it was living wood and I thought Ever Forest. I didn't think he meant Demon Spawn. No one can go there but demons."

There was silence between the two before Lily answered his obvious question, "Odolus sold a person in that village the seeds. The Minotaur you know happened upon that tree."

Captain Inertia looked at her with a grave expression, "Did Odolus have access to your case?"

Meanwhile

"Todd, it has been a while." The witch said as she came inside of the cottage.

Father Todd looked over Canting's body as he lay sleeping comfortably on the cot. The witch turned to her small cauldron and began stirring the contents inside. There was silence in the small space, as Todd looked at all the different symbols strewn across the walls with strange items or dolls. Todd really couldn't tell what most of the stuff was.

"It has," he said.

Lily came back inside shortly after a few minutes of more silence. She felt the tension between the two and chose to sit in a corner, simply to observe the two.

"How have you been?" The witch asked.

"I came here to ask for a potion to get rid of my nightmares," Father Todd stated.

The witch looked at him with a frown and then muttered underneath her breath, "When did I give birth to a chicken?" "What?" Father Todd asked. "Why do you need the potion?"

"To get rid of my nightmares." He stated with exhausted irritation.

"What are your nightmares?"

"My village dying before my eyes."

"There is no potion for that." The witch stated with a smile, "But there is a cure."

The witch walked over to Father Todd, who wasn't paying attention to her.

"Can you make the cure?" he asked.

"Sure." She smacked him across the back of his head,

"Grow up, baby."

Father Todd grabbed his head in pain and turned around to begin yelling but she cut him off.

"The world is at war, little Todd. Thousands of creatures are just like you right now and they have the willingness to stand up, trying to resist the tide of destruction," she said, looking him in the eyes, "You think self-pity fixed the world? You think wiping out painful memories made kings? You have pain, we all have pain, and we all have to deal with it.

You are a man of God, so go talk to your God. Stop crying like a child and be a man."

Father Todd stood there, speechless as she walked back to her cauldron.

"You see that little tree goblin? Who saved that tree goblin? Who, in the middle of war, had the bravery to properly coat and cover his wounds? Who prevented a vampire from dying?" she asked.

Father Todd looked at her and Lily could see the transformation in his eyes, "Me."

"That's the cure. You want to repent for what you let happen? You want the pain to go away? Make it go away. Do so many good deeds that you no longer feel that the mere thought of what happened that day could kill you. That is the cure. That is your potion and only you can make."

There was more silence as Father Todd enveloped himself within his thoughts. His memories were no longer able to cripple him and he was surprised at how that small speech made by a one-eyed witch could have been so profound on him.

Lily Trotter continued to watch the transformation take place and she felt a small sense of pride begin to well up in her. One speech from one mother changed the world of one child. It was more powerful than any magic ever created, the ability to turn darkness into light at its very core.

Father Todd looked over at Lily for a moment before he asked, "Who are you?"

Lily smiled, "I am Lily Trotter."

"What do you do, Lily?"

Lily smiled maliciously, "I weed out the useless and take back the useful."

She saw the flicker of fear in his eyes before he continued,

"So, are you the protector of this island?"

The witch and her looked at each other for a moment, and then burst out laughing, "No, I'm not the protector. I am an Angelic Detective."

Father Todd looked at her for a moment and she could see the gears turning in his head. His eyes flickered towards the upward left to access biblical references while moving right to fill in the blanks. His hand twitched as his mind reformed the mental barrier of acceptance he had previously built. His tongue began to lick his lip, the usual sign that he would be talking about a subject that was sensitive to him but he needed to satiate his curiosity.

"Angelic Detective... so you're from Heaven's Gate?"

Lily scrunched her eyebrows and nodded her head in approval, "So you know about Heaven's Gate then?"

"I know only what Captain Inertia told me."

"Yes, I am an Angelic Detective from Heaven's Gate."

"What is your purpose as a detective?"

"I have been assigned with the task of rooting out and finding the connection between everything that is happening in the world right now."

"That's kind of like figuring out the plan of God, is it not? What's so big that it's taking place all over the world and is noticeable enough that a detective is required?"

"No, I do not know if God has a plan or not. If Captain Inertia told you about Heaven's Gate then he must have surely told you what took place on your island." Lily began and, seeing Father Todd nod, she continued, "Heaven and Hell have forces that are trying to find the Medal of Scalon but the werewolves made an incalculable move with your island. Along with many other regions of the world, there were shadow ghosts that helped maintain the balance and structure of the world. Werewolves and vampires were an unforeseen creation that took place with a ton of black magic and demonic power. They are the only two species on the planet that were not intended creations. Even demons were made with a purpose.

The werewolves used a demon to capture the four shadow ghosts that maintained balance in the world and now the world is out of sorts. Magicians used to have a cap to their power and now there is none. Vampires could not walk outside while it was dark and now the strongest of them can. Humans have begun to exhibit unnatural powers or abilities and the things that went bump in the night are now coming out in the day. Right now, the world is in an absolute mess because of the werewolves.

It is my job as the Angelic Detective to root out the sources, causes, and leads to this problem. The flower that you hold contains forbidden magic, which is why it is so rare. It was created to teach those who try to capture it the folly of having too much power. As you could see, the enemy just handed the flower over without a second thought.

This flower, in the wrong hands, could devastate many parts of the world with the simplest spells. Advanced magic is no longer needed so long as you can make a good rhyme; magic is so simple that goblins can cast more than one spell now."

Father Todd listened intently and once Lily was done, he asked, "So, what are you?"

"I am an angel, a vampire, a werewolf, and a ghost," Lily said.

"How did that happen?"

"Kentro, out there, is technically my father. Traditionally, one becomes a werewolf if they are bitten but one can also become a werewolf if the father of the child is a werewolf as well. Vampires, on the other hand, work off of blood. So, even if you only get a drop of vampire blood in your veins, you will become a vampire.

My mother, the previous Angelic Detective, was an angel that was sent to see how the negotiations between the werewolf clans were going. They have been unstable since their creation and there are a few brands of werewolves that simply haven't been able to get past their differences. Kentro and my mother, Eson Trotter, had fallen in love over the many times that she watched his leader converse with the other clan leaders. My mother was married to angel that had ascended from being a vampire, which is to say that they are a vampiric angel. Many vampires try to do good deeds in their life to make up for their transgressions as a blood-sucking fiend and my *father* was one of them. This was an arranged marriage to prevent fighting amongst the varieties of angels in Heaven's Gate.

My vampiric father came home to see my mother pregnant and a fight between them ensued as the story of my parents' affair came into light. As a final act of aggression before being locked up, my father forced his blood into my mother. This turned her into a vampiric angel who was having a werewolf child. At that point in time, the blood of two angels, a vampire, and a werewolf were all in my blood stream.

The unique aspect of my situation made the demons of Demon Spawn very uneasy, knowing that I would have the best of nearly everything. One day, my mother was spending time with both of my father's when I wondered off. As you can see, I'm not exactly large and this is because I was twelve when I died. The demons managed to find me while I wandered off and I was killed.

"A couple of hundred years later, Heaven and Hell go psycho when they realize the werewolves were making a power grab. They needed a being that could hold their own with all four races so that they could figure out how everything was happening, why it was happening, and how to prevent the world from being obliterated as the Medal of Scalon was still lost. That's when the two spiritual kingdoms chose to raise me out of my grave as a manifested ghost and that's how I came to be who I am.

"I can travel into every area on Earth without any magic being able to interfere with my work."

"Wow, that's a rough story. I still don't know who my parents are."

The witch sat in front of Father Todd and grabbed his hand, "Listen, Todd."

"Yes?" Father Todd asked uncomfortably.

The witch held her breath and then let out a sigh, "I am your mother."

Father Todd placed his hand on hers, "I know you're like my mother but I still don't know my real parents. I appreciate everything you have done for me over my life, raising me in my village and only moving out when I turned to the church." The witch shook her head, "No, I understand that this may be confusing for you. I asked the church to take you so that you were not forced to assume my role. Witchcraft is not universally accepted. I am your mother, Todd."

Father Todd's mouth opened in shock, "Who is my father?"

Captain Inertia was placing the planks on the ship while Kentro was bringing more lumber. The first bit was to get the ship back together and, to his surprise, there wasn't that much damage. The most damage was at the front and top of the ship. They had been working as fast as they could to make sure they finished the boat by sun down so that the captain could go into his cabin, which had sun spells all throughout the room already.

Captain Inertia took a break from the work as he finished fixing the hole in the deck and his crew finished up his room. He beckoned them all to come forward and began to call out the names of his crew. Many of the men and women he had once known to run his ship was now dead, and he had just enough to keep the ship sailing but there would be no regular pirating as they had done in the past. There simply wasn't enough sword power to carry it out.

"This does not bode well with sailing out, Captain." Kentro stated.

"Alright, listen up mates. Kentro is now my first mate. He was there when the portal was made and he assured victory for all of us by holding off the demons on the other side of the gate. We all worked together as we should but he is the reason why you were not overwhelmed by sheer power in the end, and he is the reason I am still alive.

Most of the ship has been damaged and we only had enough wood to fix the important areas. We will be heading to the Academy of Magic at early dawn, so I want you all to room somewhere and be ready for a swift sailing. The ship will make it until we get there and then we can fix the rest of what's wrong with our baby. Better yet, we may be able to recruit some of the Knighthood to fill our open spots as we travel to Heaven's Gate," he said as he looked at his crew, "Now, there's something I want you to know. You are my family, you are my friends, and this is why I will warn you ahead of time." He pointed to the graves of the traitors.

"They were all loyal men, they were my family and your family, and they were your friends and my friends. However, they shared a loyalty to someone else and that is where they ended up."

He paused to make sure all the eyes of his crew were on them.

"We have the most valuable assets in the world travelling with us in the morning. The Angelic Detective, the Flower of Endless Spells, and a creature so powerful that it has not been given a name yet. They are our cargo and they are our responsibility, MY responsibility. They are what will save the world. So if any of you have a similar loyalty, do not come aboard my ship tomorrow for it will be a death sentence. Do not bother with good byes; do not bother with tears, for those of us who remained truthfully loyal to *The Vile Jewel.* You were never truly one of us and you should no longer pretend to be. That is all."

Captain Inertia watched sun come over the horizon and he saw a black spec become illuminated.

"Kentro, where is my spyglass?" Captain Inertia asked.

"It's in your cabin, sir."

Captain Inertia walked to his cabin and rummaged around in what was left of his dresser. He pulled out his long golden spyglass, which was buried underneath the captain's logs. He came back outside and began to climb the bird's peak carefully, his body still slightly weak from the battle. The last thing he needed right now was a new enemy and for his body to give out.

He landed atop the peak and pointed his spyglass out towards the horizon at the black spec. It was another pirate ship that was sailing towards the island with the flag raised. The symbol on it was of a red phoenix surrounded by a purple cloud.

"Friendly pirates in sight!" Captain Inertia called out.

"Who is it, sir?" Kentro yelled up at him.

"It's *The Phoenix Plague*," Captain said as he looked down at them.

"You think that might join in our adventure?"

"No, they'd plunder whatever we had at this point. However, from their distance, they won't make it until morning. They wouldn't want to plunder the witch village… or, at least, I don't think they're stupid enough. Either way, we don't have the fighting force to take them with our ship. Just keep an eye out for them at night. If any trouble happens, inform the Angelic Detective, she'll take care of it," he said as he looked at them again from the spyglass.

He climbed back down, but noticed something on the way down. Another group of ships were on the opposite shore line of them.

Looking through the spyglass while positioning his arm as an anchor, Captain Inertia watched them. Most of them wore green armour that was non-reflecting and they all had long hair.

"Great, elves."

He watched them as they began to take armaments out of their cargo bays and many of them were in the process of building catapults. A small army had landed and now they were fortifying the beach, making their siege weapons movable.

The elves were an unusual sight here because they were supporters of magic and, for a small army like, this was generally unheard of in magic based villages. They supported magic but they didn't defend magic.

"Where is the bleed hearts general?" Captain Inertia whispered underneath his breath.

Each general inside of the elven army had a purpose, a specific employment. There were many generals of the same type but all of them had specific distinctions. Defender, Attacker, Ambusher, and Espionage were the four classes. This came in handy when you knew their army and whether or not they were there to spy on you, attack you, or defend you. The elven army was the largest army on the planet with most of its forces made up of hardened veterans that simply did not die. They were also borderline crazy when it came to morals but that was because most of them had seen nothing more than war, and immortality just made things worse.

There he was, covered in green army with a single blue ribbon on the side of his right arm. Standing there amongst the soldiers, General Grey was pointing at a map to his lieutenants. This man was a "Second Star Defender" and that meant good and bad things. The first bit meant that no matter what hit them, they would most likely live. The last bit meant that whatever they had come here to defend against was big enough that they needed their next best general to defend, so it would eat Captain Inertia's crew alive.

He took his eye out of the spyglass and slid down the pole to the deck of the ship. Instantly, he yelled out to his crew, "Everybody up! We need to move the ship now!"

"But sir, we just repaired her. Don't you think the crew deserves a breather?" Kentro asked.

Captain Inertia looked at him and shook his head, "You'll understand the order in a moment. Everyone, get this ship to the other side of the island and make ready for departure."

The crew groaned their complaints but followed the orders. Within minutes, the ship was smoothly sailing to the other side of the island where the troops were. Kentro let out a groan finally as he saw the general.

The general came over to greet them.

"What business does *The Vile Jewel* have here?" General Grey asked.

Kentro jumped off of the moving ship and looked at the troops that were now completing their tasks. It was almost sunset and the captain would have to resign himself to his cabin to make sure that he wasn't swallowed by the darkness.

"We have living cargo in the village. Legal transport." Captain Inertia called out, "What business does a Second Star have here?"

With one word, Captain Inertia's spine became frozen with ice, "Sarnia."

"Sarnia is coming out of hiding again? For what?" Captain Inertia asked.

General Grey looked at Captain Inertia with suspicion, "What living cargo do you have here? Disclose what you are doing before I give you the answers of what I'm doing."

Captain Inertia made a long sigh because he knew this would take the night up for the most part, "Come into my cabin so I don't die, General."

Meanwhile...

Kentro looked at the weapons that the troops had and all of it seemed to indicate what type of enemy might show up. Silver spears, silver swords, silver laden boulders, and enough silver shining on their armour to make a small kingdom jealous.

"So, they think Sarnia and a legion of werewolves will be attacking this point? For what, and how are they here at the same time as us? This is too strange to be coincidence." Kentro thought.

He made his way to the witch's place where Father Todd and Lily were still talking. As he opened the door, a silence fell over the room as he looked at the two.

"Lily, the elven army is here." Kentro stated.

"Of course they are, how do you think I got here?" Lily asked sarcastically.

"Anyway, you were saying about Casimpra?" The witch asked.

"Before I came to this island, I was supposed to pass on a message to a shadow master at shore's end but Captain Inertia told me that the shadow master was dead," Father Todd stated.

"He lied," Kentro said bluntly.

"What?" Father Todd asked.

"The shadow master is still alive but, ever since the war began, the enemy has been trying to find him. He's one of the most prominent knowledge seekers in the world and surpassed the limits of magic before the shadow ghosts were captured. If anyone can find the Medal of Scalon, it'd be him, which is why they're searching so hard for him," Kentro pointed out.

"What is the Medal of Scalon?" Father Todd asked.

"It's a collection of poems." A weak voice said.

"No, little tree goblin, go back and take your rest. Those burn marks will not heal immediately, I only have a full body healing spell, and I used it for my son," the witch said.

"I will but I need to tell Father Todd this before he decides anything," Canting said.

"You stopped speaking in rhyme," Father Todd pointed out.

"That's because I'm no longer casting spells," Canting said as he let his vines hang off of the bed, "I need to cast spells to keep my normal form and it's best just to constantly cast it rather than forget, and be killed."

"So this is what a tree goblin looks like?" Lily Trotter asked.

"No, this is what I look like. There's a reason why I was in that forest by myself. Anyway, the Medal of Scalon is a medal of sorts that has poems inscribed on it. Many people don't know if the Medal is a single piece of metal or more than one piece, it's just that old. Poems are the oldest form of magic and it's how creatures found out there was magic. These poems represent the six prominent races of the world, a poem for each race. The Medal of Scalon is so powerful that whoever holds or wields it can decide the fate of the world. No one has a clue why the werewolves have been trying to make a power grab, which is why Lily Trotter has been...created?" Canting shrugged, "However, the Medal of Scalon is so old that only those of the shadow can read it. Shadow is an underground hierarchy of extremely powerful magic users, given such power either through entitlement with responsibility or sheer will power. Only the ranks of shadow ghosts and shadow masters are known."

"Wow, that sounds like a handful of death," Father Todd said with a nervous laugh but no one laughed at him.

Kentro looked at his daughter, "Captain Inertia told me to inform you of anything that might go wrong. The elven army is building armaments and there's a pirate ship on its way here that will arrive in the morning depending on its intentions."

Lily nodded, "I know about the pirate ship. I requested that they meet us here in case of complications with the demons aboard Captain Inertia's ship, a failsafe of sorts. Regardless, they can provide the manpower that *The Vile Jewel* is now lacking."

"They also said that Sarnia is coming." Kentro stated gravely.

"Who is Sarnia?" Father Todd asked.

Lily's eyes expanded, "She's the demon that captured the shadow ghosts."

Outside, the noise of the bugs and night creatures filled the air. Father Todd listened to Lily as she went through all the cases she had investigated since she had been brought back. He was interested to see how her description of Heaven was completely detailed compared to what he had taught in his small village.

The night fire burn brilliantly and it seemed as though fire imps were dancing in front of his eyes as he was enthralled in the epics of Lily Trotter. In a slight disturbance, the door opened and Captain Inertia walked into the cottage.

"What brings a vampire in the darkness?" Lily asked.

"We need to find out where we are going," Captain Inertia said in a haggard voice as he held his lantern aloft to beat away the darkness.

"I thought vampires loved the darkness?" Father Todd asked curiously.

Lily chuckled, "Those are to keep the children from going out of their bedrooms at night and from teens wandering into shady areas. The truth is that vampires loathe the darkness and the less light there is then the less the vampire is alive. That's why they always carry an Eternal Flame candle from birth and Mr. Inertia has it in his lantern."

"That's Captain Inertia to you, ghost," Inertia said with a slightly angry glint.

"That's MISTER Inertia or would you like me to steal your ship again?" Lily asked, snidely.

"You got lucky," Inertia said with a half-hearted smile.

"Then I've gotten lucky every time you've insisted that I call you Captain Inertia. You're no longer a captain in my eyes. That stopped the day that you and *The Vile Jewel* were cursed by the sea wench," Lily stated with crossed arms.

"What makes it so urgent that planning our route couldn't wait until morning?" Canting asked.

Captain Inertia smiled, "You pick up quick, little goblin. The elven army believes that Sarnia may come and there so happens to be a well-known pirate shore supposedly coming in friendly tomorrow."

Lily crossed her arms, "Isn't our path a little obvious? We need to head to the Academy of Magic in order ensure a path to Heaven's Gate."

Captain Inertia raised an eyebrow, "That's a very nice path but I'd like to head to the Ever Tree Forest to check on the Minotaur village that accidently sold me that wood. Any demon can make a portal from that wood and they are a peaceful people."

Lily smiled, "That's awfully sweet of you Captain Inertia but Heaven has made my directive clear. We must converse with the Council of Shadows so that you all can gain access into Heaven's Gate. They have *requested* your audience."

Captain Inertia, "Hmph, requested? More like demand."

Lily shrugged, "I could always authorize a B unit and then you would be captives of war. Would you like to be tortured with various and creative ways?"

Father Todd's mouth was open in shock, "Why are you two making Heaven sound so horrible?"

Lily cocked her head to the side, "Heaven is neither a horrible place nor is it a fantastic place. It's Heaven, it's whatever they want it to be."

"But I teach that Heaven is where all the good souls go," Father Todd stated.

"That's not a lie." Lily nodded, "That is entirely true."

"Then how can you make Heaven sound so horrible?

Torture, war units, detectives…those are all Earth things!" Father Todd said grabbing his head.

"Heaven is the creator of evil. Why would it not have areas of it inside of Heaven?" Lily asked bluntly.

"Because it's Heaven, the source of all good!" Father Todd screamed.

"Does your book say that?" Lily asked.

Father Todd began flipping through the pages but could not find anything. He began to sob horribly as he let the book fall from his hands and his tears dripped onto the floor.

The witch came over, "This is why I couldn't let you follow my path without choosing your own. The truths of this world can be harsh some times."

She grabbed her son and held his head towards her chest. He cried uncontrollably as the rest of them stood in silence.

"Shh, now. Heaven is truly a source for all the good in the world but it cannot stay good if they do not treat evil as it is." The witch said as she comforted Todd, "Your book did not say that because it was chosen not to be put in. Even evil can read the book and good must keep secrets if it is to stay alive. It *is* a kingdom of its own after all."

Father Todd began to control his crying and he slowly stopped. The world was coming into balance for him.

Lily shrugged, "That's a gentler way of explaining it but it's all true. Heaven has a military, a wall of sorts, and the king of all kings. So, why would we not have the tools to operate a kingdom? It is quite a pleasant place in the inner city. Although it's a little creepy for my tastes; everything that was described in your book is there but the more sensitive parts of our home abode were left out for purposes of war."

Captain Inertia laughed, "It's like the royal army pamphlet for humans. Where they tell you about all the good bits but when you join, you see that there are definitely things you know weren't in the pamphlet."

"Anyway, there are issues at hand that must be dealt with. What path will we take to the Academy of Magic?" Canting asked.

It was unnerving to see the tree goblin not speaking in rhyme but it was a relief that he was continuously blunt and his words weren't clouded by riddles.

"We will take the Blood Styx River," Captain Inertia stated, opening the map on the witch's coffee table.

Lily shook her head, "It would be easier to navigate the Moon Stone river."

"Yes, but that would mean we would have more potential threats." Captain Inertia pointed out.

"Potential threats are of no concern to me. We head to Heaven's Gate through the Academy of Magic, I will take care of any who pose a threat," Lily stated with a shrug.

Captain Inertia crossed his arms, "My lady, Angelic Detective, there are things in this world that even you cannot kill."

Lily smiled, "The day I meet one is the day I become mortal again."

Captain Inertia pointed a finger at Lily, "You forget there are shadow masters that can perform such a spell."

Lily shrugged, "I suppose it's good that you came in with your maps. We also need to charter our way to the Shadow Ghosts."

"Why would we need to go to them?"

"We need to free the Shadow Ghosts in order to obtain the location of the Medal of Scalon, the reason why I exist right now," Lily stated, "Unless you want to lose your status as C.I. for Heaven and see the world in flames, you may want help save the world by being an escort."

Captain Inertia burst out laughing, "If the world is destroyed because we can't find a medallion, there's no Heaven anyway."

Lily smiled, "That's the point but you do need to make sure that the Flower of Endless Spells makes it to Heaven's Gate. It's the only magic left that can save the Shadow Ghosts from Sarnia's grip."

"That'll be interesting to watch," Captain Inertia stated.

Father Todd lifted his head, "But I thought I could use the flower to get a potion to clear my mind. I figured it was a symbol of power."

"The honest truth is that I would fear the flower would bring unwanted attention." The witch stated, "I'm sure you had no ill intentions but such a flower would easily give the enemy an advantage. Sense the flower never dies and it can supply the user with limitless power, a leader would be able to conquer kingdoms with it. If the enemy ever got a hold of this flower, it would mean the end of any opposition we could pose to those who would use the Medal of Scalon for ill purposes."

"I see what you mean," Father Todd said with a nod.

"Plus, a potion made with this flower would wipe your memory not just **a** memory. You would become a vegetable and the unique experience that you had would not be put to good use." Lily pointed out.

"Oh, I'm not interested in wiping my memory any more. Mom convinced me of that," Father Todd said with a nervous laugh.

"So, we'll take the Moon Stone River," Captain Inertia said as he rolled up the map.

"Wait, what about the Shadow Ghosts?" Lily asked.

Captain Inertia smiled maliciously and shrugged, "We'll figure it out on the way."

Lily grabbed Inertia by the cuff, "No, it must all be planned."

"No it mustn't," Captain Inertia said, licking is his lips.

"Yes it does!" Lily said pulling on Inertia's cheek.

"No it doesn't!" Inertia said, pushing her face with his hand in order to get her off.

The two continued to fight as Father Todd and the witch fought.

"Do these two normally act like this?" Father Todd asked.

"Yes, the captain and Lily are like siblings because her father works on his ship. She's a perfectionist that overanalyses everything and he's a man that loves to nitpick at people's pet peeves in general. From what her father says, it provides the crew with non-stop entertainment during visits." The witch said with an awkward smile.

"Alright, Lily, I must get back to the crew. We'll talk about this after morning comes because we don't know which way we might need to escape to." Captain Inertia pointed out, pulling away from her.

Lily stood up and straightened her coat, "Fine. If Sarnia truly does show up, it'd be best to have all options open to us. Inform the crew that we might have a war in the morning. I don't want them to be caught off guard like the time the sirens ate half of your crew while they were sleeping."

Captain Inertia scratched the back of his head, "Yeah, I had no idea they would do something that foolish."

Captain Inertia grabbed his charts and left the cottage.

Everything had quieted down when Father Todd looked over at Canting. Many of the bandages had turned brown and most of them needed changed. Canting lay in the bed with his breath laboured from that day's intense battle.

"Do you have any first aid material?" Father Todd asked the witch.

The witch got up and opened up a cabinet. Looking inside, she pulled out a roll of bandages and some liquor.

"I never planned on taking care of living plants but this should do. He's a tree, so it's not like he can get sick but it will be a few days before his wounds will fully heal." The witch stated.

"How is a creature like him brought into the world?" Father Todd asked as he grabbed the bandages and the alcohol from him.

"Trees are living, it's just that they have no need for mouths. Goblins mated with the tree nymphs of the Ever forest...through, horrible means of course. Many nymphs had unusual mixtures as children and left them abandoned. Over a few centuries, these abandoned creatures came together in small pockets and began producing children of their own.

Many of them hide behind magic and are peaceful, so it's rare to see an actual tree goblin in its normal form."

"Ah."

Father Todd bandaged Canting and sat next to him while the tree goblin put his hand on Father Todd's arm. Canting looked up at him with sympathetic eyes.

"I wish I didn't have to do this but I want you to know this before we sailed out tomorrow. Just in case we got into trouble," Canting said.

"What is it, Canting?" Father Todd asked as the witch took what remained and put it back into her cabinet.

"You are a white mage," Canting bluntly stated.

"What?" Father Todd asked in confusion.

"You are a man of God, yes?" Canting asked Father Todd in a leading manner.

"Yes."

"The book you carry is a basic understanding for how to use white magic," Canting pointed out.

"What?" Father Todd asked as he pulled out his book.

"I believe there's a son of God in there. Fell what his in your heart and ask for him to heal me," Canting stated.

"I've done that before, it only alleviates the mind," Father Todd said.

"Close your eyes. Feel your heart. Now feel the words inside of your heart and believe they are coming out of your mouth. The words will naturally follow."

Father Todd closed his eyes and imagined feeling his heart. It was warm, comforting, and had a steady beat to it. He saw the words forming over his heart and they flew out of his throat.

"Lord, let life flow through my hands and heal my friend," Father Todd said in a strange voice he'd never heard come from his mouth.

A warm feeling came from his hands and Father Todd slowly opened his eyes. A white glow was coming from his hands and it was travelling through Canting's body. Before his eyes, Canting's wound began to close and the scratches were no longer visibly. The white glow stopped and Canting sat up, pulling off the bandages.

"Many of the white mages in the world began as pastors who realized that God gave them the book to heal the weak," Canting stated, "Pastors guide the sheep in this world and the book helps protect those sheep from the wolves."

"I thought you had to have some innate ability in order to use magic," Father Todd stated.

Canting smiled, "Nope. Anyone can use magic but you have to be given the basics or else it'll just flop. Magic comes from the heart and if it comes from anywhere else then it's usually accompanied by a personal sacrifice. This is because the personal item as imbued emotions and spiritual connections to you that are powerful enough to be considered a replica you. The more powerful the outward spell the more powerful the magic itself needs to be, which is why magical items are made."

"So, like a wizard's staff is made of spiritual power?" Father Todd asked.

"The number one thing that nearly all magic users do is meditate. This is because meditating allows you to channel your magic into an item. On the go spells, like healing, take time. However, if you channel your spiritual energy into an object then you can release as much as you need in a blast. This would let you heal or even revive an entire army if you spent the proper amount of time to store the spiritual energy. Crystals are the best for receiving magic," Canting said, "Speaking of which, place your hand over your book and kindly ask your God to unlock it."

Father Todd did as Canting asked and the book glowed with light for a moment before a large black crystal showed on top.

"Ooooh, you have one of the rare books. That's a black crystal, which reflects the endless night. In other words, there's no limit to how much you can put in there," Canting stated with a pleased smile, "You can pull it out and use what you've stored in it to do *whatever* you want. White magic simply means that you use magic from Heaven and you can use for anything but remember to keep Heaven's rules on magic in mind. No murder and things like that but it's useful for defense. Eventually you can put your own in it but the white magic will be limitless. All you have to do is ask for your crystal to be filled."

"Wow, that's a lot to absorb and I only have one question," Father Todd said in surprise.

"What's that?" Canting asked.

"Why would anyone turn to black magic? I assume that comes from Demon Spawn," Father Todd asked.

"No, black magic comes from Hell Gate. They turn to it because you can do dirty things with it. Murder, thought manipulation, and plenty of other things considered as bad," Canting said, "Your mother uses a variety of magic. There's a rainbow of colours but you can learn more about that later. Just focus on using what magic you have so that it can be used in case of an emergency. If we head to Hell Gate and you haven't learned the variations then I will teach you but I'd rather stay away from that."

"Just taking all of this in is just completely mind-blowing. Everything I've believed to be true is on a side track of what it really is," Father Todd said with a sigh.

"Yeah, that will happen a lot on this adventure of ours. The truths of the world are skewed to serve the needs of others," Canting said.

"That's kind of pointless," Father Todd stated.

"If you tell someone they're going to be tortured by creatures that live on torture because you didn't do something right and they are someone with power, will you not listen?" Canting said.

"Well… only if I believe what they say," Father Todd stated.

"Exactly the point. Your religion has only lasted so long because there's truth and belief in it," Canting stated.

"Wow," Father Todd said as his thoughts swirled around him.

"So, where is all this shadow stuff coming from?" Father Todd asked after a long moment of silence.

"Shadow stuff?" Lily asked.

"Yeah. So far, I've heard of Shadow Master and Shadow Ghost, and that you need to achieve a point where your magic breaks the barriers… but…what does it mean?"

Lily laughed, "All this talk about magic and how to use it. It's like teaching a newborn how to breathe." Father Todd gazed at her with a frown.

"Alright, alright. Listen close because I'm only going to do this once," Lily said. "Shadow refers to the inner soul and – depending on the leftover amount of your soul – you are given a title that explains how far gone you are. Shadow Ghosts are basically mages who have used their souls completely for the soul purpose of magic. The original Shadow Ghosts used their souls to balance the world, which basically forced them into immortality while taking their souls. They cannot be killed unless the balance they used to help the world is destroyed itself. Shadow Masters basically means that the person has infused so much of their soul into objects around the world that they are unable to part from the world until those objects are destroyed," Lily stated, "Do you have any coffee? The rest of this conversation may take a while."

"Of course, I got addicted to it whenever I took care of my son. Helps alleviate the constant irritation of children and people, you know?" The witch said laughing.

Lily nodded and then turned back to Father Todd, "As Canting explained to you, magic comes from spiritual power. Most spiritual users use power that's given to them by their deity. There are many deities around the world that supply their mages with spiritual power. However, their spiritual power is dependent on their followers, unlike God. The more followers that they have, the more Heavenly Boon they receive. Now, all these deities give away their magic so that the individual doesn't have to use their own. This is because soul magic is immortal and can only be transported as a single item. In other words, unless your soul is in one piece, you can't ascend or descend. This is a two-edged sword for most who want to stay in this world or want to escape judgment."

Father Todd nodded, "So, even if a sliver of soul has been separated from the body, it will prevent you from *actually dying.*"

"In a way. The soul fragments will stay alive in the objects where you put them. Now, Shadow, means that you can't go to purgatory. Purgatory is a place where impartial or incomplete souls go to get repaired. It's a place for mages and people who didn't realize that they gave off some of their soul, and now they need to be made whole before they can fully die. So, you can still get into Heaven or Hell without waiting until the bits of your soul in the world are collected. Purgatory just repairs what is missing."

"So Shadow Masters aren't allowed into Purgatory?" Father Todd asked with his right eyebrow raised.

"There's a weight scale in the universe and souls weigh a certain amount. Or I should say that souls have an opposite weight. This is really confusing, so I'll try to explain this bit the best I can. When you have a full soul, it weighs the exact amount it needs to in order to go straight to God. It's an extremely light weight. The less soul you have, the heavier it is, and the less distance the soul is able to travel to. When you do bad things, it literally kills part of the soul because it's a piece of God but it doesn't make your soul heavier. When you go to your judgment, God is deciding whether or not he wants the piece back or if it should go in the trash."

"So…Shadow means…a shadow of what was once a soul?" Father Todd asked.

"You hit it on the nail," Lily said as she sipped her coffee.

"Wasn't it against God to follow other gods?" Father Todd asked.

"Deities are not gods and they have followers, not worshippers. Deities are Shadow Masters that choose to serve as magical fountains for the magical world instead of keeping a corporeal form. As a reward for their service, they receive something called a Heavenly Boon. Which is to say that they have access to something exclusively rare called the World Soul and have limitless power. For every follower that they have, they receive another Heavenly Boon. Each Heavenly Boon boosts the magic power of its users and the amount of power a user can obtain is rather mind boggling. However, there are stipulations and guidelines that have to be followed," Lily stated.

"Like what?"

"Hmm…let's use the Sasha Deity for example, or better known to its pupils as the Moon Deity. The stipulation to the Moon Deity is that the users will only be as strong as the amount of moonlight that is covering the ground. In other words, Moon Deity followers will be unstoppable on a full moon but powerless during the day."

"Why wouldn't they just follow God?"

"They are, just in a different way and means. In addition, God only grants power to those in true need. Otherwise, it's just magic for healing and nothing else. The Paladin Order love following Exodus, or the Light Deity, which is another form of white magic. However, their stipulation is that you must follow the Code of Honour and you are only given a specific amount of power per your rank."

"So, I'm basically still a pastor but I can heal my friends?" Father Todd asked, "I can see how that can be useful." "You can also Recall souls," Canting stated.

"Recall?"

"Basically, you can call the soul of the people who died to come back to their bodies to carry out what they were meant to do. Nearly every major city has at least one devout pastor so that if the city is ever in need, the pastor can use this power to consistently bring back the dead to defend the innocent citizens. Pastors are also the only mages in the world that can restore a Shadow Master's soul so that they can go to Heaven or Hell and they are the only ones in the world that can save a starving nation."

"You make being a Pastor sound cool," Father Todd said with a laugh.

Lily nodded and smiled, "Devout pastors, the ones in it to save and help people, are considered national treasures by intelligent kingdoms. Although, it's difficult to stay a devout pastor when people shower you with praises, give you gifts, and free meals. A few pastors I know of have used this to further help those in need and even more have used it to hold a position of power over people." Lily pointed out.

"Being a pastor means giving up yourself to God and staying strong so that others may lean on you. It's saddening to hear that so many have fallen to evil by simply doing what they thought was right and being corrupted by Earthly treasures," Father Todd stated as he gently felt the crystal on the front of his book.

"Spoken like a true pastor," Lily said with a smile.

"Although I have a nagging question that's been in the back of my head ever since I was told that the Shadow Master was dead. Why did Cassimpra just hand me the flower of Endless Spells if she could have just used it to find the Shadow Master she was looking for?" Father Todd asked.

Lily let out a huge sigh as she put her cup of coffee on the table, "Cassimpra is more interested in finding the Shadow Master than anyone else. Currently, she's employed by Demon Spawn to find him and has the ability to use demon magic. This allows her to protect herself from the normal hazards that vampires face during the night time. However, demon magic cannot be used to locate those who have no soul. Even if she were to use the flower, it would serve no purpose because his body is a shell. The truth is that he has known for a while that she has been looking for him because he knows the location of the Medal of Scalon. He also happens to be her father from the time they both followed the Blood

Deity," Lily stated, "Captain Inertia lied to you because it would have been best if you did not find him. That particular Shadow Master has a weakness for pastors who seem lost and if you had sought him out, there would have been a good chance that he would have come out of hiding."

"If he knows the location of the Medal of Scalon, then why wouldn't you be searching for him right now?" Father Todd asked, "Getting it before the bad guys is usually the good guys job."

"No, my job is to find out the locations of the Shadow Ghosts and free them from their prisons. The Medal of Scalon is a side-job. More of a job like *meh, if you find it, that'd be nice* ordeal. I am here to find the culprits behind the disorder in the world more than I am here to find the one thing the enemy wants so that it's in plain view for whomever might want to take it. It's easier to hide something from the enemy when you don't even know where it is."

"Do you know where they are?"

Lily shrugged, "I've got a general idea of where they were last."

"How is that helpful?"

"Shadow Ghosts move when they want to. Not even Sarnia's bottles have enough magic to move them because they can make themselves weigh as much as they want to without being crushed. I have to assume that they've done so to prevent them being taken to a place where Heaven cannot find them," Lily stated, "Although, one of them is in Demon Spawn, which will be hard like hell to get into."

"If you need special access to Heaven's Gate, don't you need special access to Demon Spawn?" Father Todd asked.

Lily burst out laughing and fell on the floor, tears rolling from her eyes. She struggled to stand back up and wiped the tears off of her face.

"Can you ever imagine a demon hiding?" Lily asked.

"No, not really."

"Then why would they place requirements for those who wish to enter and make a challenge to a force that thinks that all the world, including Heaven, should be bowing before their feet?" Lily smiled.

"No, that wouldn't make sense. But why did Cassimpra join Demon Spawn if her father is supposed to be a good guy?"

"I grew up with her and she's not the type to back down. When Heaven told her to stop looking for him and cut off her magic when she tried to do so without permission, she turned to Demon Spawn who more than happily agreed to supply her with magic power," Lily stated.

"How did you grow up with her?"

"She's my sister, technically."

"What?!"

"Remember how I told you that I'm a vampire's daughter through blood? Cassimpra is the legitimate child of that father. I am the legitimate child of a werewolf. As historical puns go, we've always been at odds with each other. I had a happy childhood while she had one filled with greed, it makes for a good war," Lily said as she picked her teeth.

"That's the most confusing circle of enemies that I've ever seen," Father Todd said with a slight chuckle.

"Truly but I know that she is only using the Demon Spawn magic to find him. Mainly because she's had him most of her life and then he just up, and disappeared. Mostly, she's pissed."

"How will you deal with her when you face her?"

"She defied Heaven. I'll kill her of course."

"That's horrible."

"No, defying Heaven so brazenly is horrible…and stupid."

"Wouldn't you take her to Heaven's jail or something?"

"Would you treat treason so lightly? When you knew the culprit knew that finding her father would ruin the world? No, treason must be dealt with swiftly and accordingly," Lily stated.

A couple hours later

Father Todd could hear the sleeping breaths of the witch and Lily as he lay on the ground. Canting and Lily were sleeping in the extra bunk and the witch slept in her own bed. The ground was hard but it was more comfortable than the bed he had back in the church. The aching pain of his back seemed to be relieved that it no longer had to carry his body.

"Canting?" Father Todd asked quietly.

"Yes, Pastor?" Canting whispered back.

"I'm going to go outside and watch the stars."

"Why are you telling me?"

Father Todd thought about the odd question and then caught himself laughing. He had gotten so used to being mindful of his manners that he forgot who he was travelling with.

"Nevermind."

Father Todd got up and walked out of the cottage. The silence around him was only broken by the waves of the ocean.

The night stars shone down on him more brightly than ever before as his mind settled down from the crashing reality of what and who he was just moments ago. He had never really thought about who he was, God had always provided him the answer. Now he learned that the people he had refused entrance into his city years before might have very well been comrades in arms. Although, he remember quite a few of them that had an appearance that would definitely disagree with him.

The moon was beautiful over the ocean, like a soft light that looked as though it would carry him away to a peaceful land where he could just let his thoughts roam. A sudden light appeared before him in the ocean and he walked towards it without thinking. He shielded his eyes from the bright light and he could see the image of a woman in his eyes as he stumbled forward.

The light calmed down and he now saw a woman with long pale hair. Her skin was that of the moon behind her and she had dark blue eyes that seemed to hold him in a trance. His feet did not stop as he got near her and he felt his mind trying to reject the trance but his heart felt warm. He came to her and she opened her arms for him, and he found himself in her embrace.

"Who are you?" he asked softly.

"I am one that loves you. Calm your thoughts and let your mind be still," she said in a harmonic tone.

"Who are you?" he asked again softly.

"Shh, be still my love. This day has found you many friends. Let your mind be still and let me take the pain of the past from you," she said.

Father Todd remembered images and memories of his village, which seemed far away now. The day that he opened the gate for the werewolves and the massacre all came back to him. He let it go before he even realized it and began crying on her shoulder. The tears felt warm as they leaked on to her skin and he felt at peace even as the tears left his eyes. He no longer wondered who she was and didn't have a care in the world.

"Hey…pastor…it's not a good idea just to fall asleep out here." A familiar voice poked at him.

Father Todd opened his eyes and saw Canting standing before his legs. The night was clouded now and he could barely make out the stars.

"It looks like it's going to rain," Canting said as he looked at Father Todd, "I'd suggest getting back inside pastor."

The clouds above indeed looked as if it would pour at any moment. As Father Todd and Canting headed back inside, he noticed that Lily was sitting at the table again.

"What? Did everyone wake up?" he asked.

Lily smirked as she took off her hat and sipped a little more from her cup of coffee, "I'm a ghost. I don't need sleep."

Father Todd's mouth dropped as he looked at Lily and she smiled back at him. His face began to feel warm and his eyes looked away involuntarily.

"What's this? You've gone all red in the face pastor, are you sick?" Canting asked.

Father Todd felt his heart skip a beat as he felt her blue eyes watching him.

"No, Canting, I'm fine. I just need a bit of rest is all," he said with a shaking voice.

His heart was pounding so hard in his chest that he thought he might have a heart attack. The stomach was making matters much better as it rolled around with nausea and his legs felt weak. Father Todd lurched to the bed and crawled underneath its covers. He tried hard not to think about what had just happened and his hand patted his chest in hopes of calming it down enough to fall asleep. Sure enough, a few minutes later his body's exhaustion simply forced him to sleep and as the snores came out of his mouth, Lily smiled. She leaned back and put her hat back on.

"Prepare for a one-of-a-kind night, Pastor," she said as she closed her eyes.

Canting felt goose bumps as Father Todd's snores instantly stopped and his face went into a droopy smile.

"Bleh, humans," he said as he fell asleep as well.

Captain Inertia watched the elves move across the island and prepare their defenses. His pipe was beginning to taste sweet as his mouth let out another stream of smoke. Most of his crew had headed off to bed when he had told them the bad news. All of them wanted to get their sleep in for when they had to fight in the morning. Of course, their fight would be very short. It would be more on an extraction and run type of deal but most of them knew to plan for the worse. After all, Sarnia would be part of the mysterious enemy and they already had a run in with a few nasty demons in their life, Sarnia would not be one of them.

"The cannons have all been cleaned, sir," Kentro said.

"Good, good. We will need them when we run," Captain Inertia said.

"Are you sure you want to leave the island's battle to the elves? It's Sarnia. It's not like they'll stand a chance."

"You'd be surprised to find that General Grey can be a difficult man when he wants to be. They know who Sarnia wants after all, which is why a second star has come." Captain Inertia pointed out as he breathed in more of the smoke.

"Are you sure? You place so much emphasis on the fact that he's a second star." Kentro stated as he crossed his arms.

"There was a battle once, between the humans and the elves. The elves are a prideful bunch that are not easily swayed by the issues of the body, perhaps one of the more pure races to worship God. Humans, on the other, are one of the most corrupt. Second to orcs, trolls, and whatever else they have in their mishmash of a city. Demons love humans and most of the demons in this world thrive on the summons that humans do out of sinful reasons. The final battle came when the humans made a last strike at the elves, who were just about to offer humans a treaty of equality when the humans threw everything they had at the elves. Before then, humans had only contended with four star generals and had done remarkably well against the elves. However, attacking the elves main city falls under three star to one star jurisdiction. The battle was over in mere seconds and seventy percent of the human population of the world died. In one blinding move, the elves simply wiped the humans before they got a few feet from the city. Now the elves control the human populace and govern their cities so that the catastrophe never happens again. Many elves wept for the families who watched their mothers and fathers run off for a pointless cause. The shock and awe that the *elves* were all crying for the humans hit them so hard that the humans simply handed over their right to rule without even blinking," Captain Inertia stated with a slight pause of breath before asking, "Do you know what star did that?"

"A one star?" Kentro asked, shrugging his shoulders.

"His name is Three Star Attack General Kindleleaf," Captain Inertia said as he watched the rain begin to pour down outside of the ship, "There has never been a moment in history that a one star general of the elven army was called into action. The most that has even been seen was a two star general."

Kentro looked out at General Grey with new admiration, "So, that means Sarnia is as good as dead."

"I don't know. However, if the elven kingdom deems her worthy of a two star general, then my happy butt is running in the opposite direction," Captain Inertia stated.

General Grey looked back at Captain Inertia's ship and smiled. He knew the good captain would flee once their cargo was on board and the captain was relying on him to take the brunt of the force.

"Are you sure it's okay to let them dock their General? What if they provide support for the attackers from behind." His first lieutenant asked.

"It is fine. Captain Inertia has been alive long enough to know the strength of the elven army. All of you are three star generals under my command. He knows his crew isn't ready to take a single three star general, not after what he saw what happened to the humans." General Grey said as the memory of that day made his heart cringe.

"That was a truly horrid day."

"Yes, we hope never to see one like it again. We need to stop Sarnia now, which is why they asked me to come here. However, just because I'm here does not mean we can take the enemy lightly. We do not yet know the power she possesses after entrapping the Shadow Ghosts. She could very well be channelling their magic," he said.

The rain began to fall as he watched his troops move up the hill and crawl into the city. Everything was set and prepared for when the enemy should arrive before General Grey began to order campfires to keep everyone warm. Small tents were erected around the fires to keep the water off of it.

"Why was Captain Inertia there?" his first lieutenant asked after a few moments of silence.

"The human king of the main city had decided that it would be best to enact a treaty. So, believing the king had finally come to his senses, Captain Inertia escorted the king into our fair city. While in a meeting with the council, the king signed the treaty and we were all about to throw a celebration party when we heard the thunderous roar outside. The king was handcuffed and escorted outside, just in case the attack was done by humans. Captain Inertia and I were the ones who walked with him outside as the king looked out with curiosity." General Grey said as he prodded the fire in their tent, "We could all tell that the king had no idea what was going on and when we opened the doors, the look of horror that came across his face confirmed our thoughts. His kingdom had been taken over because too many humans still felt hatred towards us to let the treaty happen. Their plan was to kill us all while it was signed, even their own king. Three Star General Kindleleaf felt bad for the king and asked him if they should be captured or let go. The anger, I guess, boiled up in the king's face and tears were coming out of his eyes when he said ***kill them, wipe this human flaw off the planet***. Kindleleaf nodded and understood his wishes. He looked out over the kingdom's walls and all he did was stomp on the ground. The entire human army was squished much like you would squish a bug. Captain Inertia stayed in the kingdom to make sure the king recovered from the sight before leaving on his boat once more. It was a scar for any one of us that was there to watch it."

"And you're a two star?" his first lieutenant asked in shock.

"Yea, but I'm a Defense General," General Grey said with a smile.

"What does that mean?"

With a malicious smile and bloodlust in his eyes, General Grey replied, "Bring the enemy for dawn; I'll have a hunger for breakfast."

The sound of clashing metal could be heard from outside as Father Todd groggily woke up. The sheet that was on top of him was wet from various liquids and he found his body aching from what he thought to be oversleeping. Inside the cabin was silent and Father Todd's ears perked.

He went over to the door and opened it to the outside. He saw werewolves and elves clashing just outside of the door, with Lily and Canting fending off what they could at the door. Father Todd groaned and simply closed the door, walking back towards the counter.

"It's too early for this crap," Father Todd said as he poured himself a cup of coffee.

The aroma was robust and he could tell that the grounds had been crushed recently. With every sip, he began to wake up to what was happening outside. Before long, Father Todd feared going outside but he knew that if he was to get on the ship with the group that he would have to face it.

He put down the cup of coffee and walked back towards the door. Opening it, he saw no difference compared to what he had seen before. Lily and Canting were standing in front of the door, making sure that no enemy came near the cottage.

"Thank you for letting me sleep as long as I did," Father Todd said.

"We couldn't get you to wake up. Your body was glowing white and you were hovering the entire morning," Canting stated.

"Yes, and you made loud groaning noise that I've only ever heard from brothels," Lily stated.

Father Todd suddenly remembered what took place last night and felt his face flush again. He shook his head and attempted to regain his thoughts.

"Shouldn't we go with Captain Inertia to escape this island?" Father Todd asked.

The two of them looked at him with their mouths slightly opened and Lily laughed, "It'd be kind of rude to let the enemy kill you in your sleep, don't you think?"

"The enemy…" Father Todd found the word strange for a moment and then he began to feel a warmth inside of his hand. There lay his book, as it normally should and it was glowing a bright white inside of the crystal on the front. He didn't remember charging it but it seemed to glow brightly as he looked at it. He was lost in the light for a moment before a strange thought crossed his mind.

He giveth what he can taketh away.

Father Todd felt himself raise the book into the air and the words began to flow out of his mouth. He heard his own words and felt horrified at the words that he had said. His heart may have been sad about what happened in his village but he never thought about revenge.

"Enemies of God, I smite thee."

The words flew out of his mouth and Father Todd felt as though he was in a trance. The werewolves that had been attacking the elves simply vanished into thin air. Silence stood all around them as Lily and Canting watched with wide eyes, and the elven soldiers stood there in confusion.

There was no time for thinking as Lily grabbed his hand and they all bolted towards Captain Inertia's ship. Father Todd still felt as though he was in a trance as his mind replayed what happened over and over in his head. All three of them were silent as they passed elves who were confused as to why they had no more enemies.

General Grey looked at Father Todd and mouthed words that he would never forget, "So, this is what a horseman looks like."

Then, everything came crashing in towards Father Todd as he let go of Lily's hand and they all ran to Captain Inertia's ship. A loud crash of lightening hit the ground behind them and Father Todd caught himself looking behind them. A woman had entered the battlefield and she carried a spiked whip with her. One crack from the whip on the ground sent the elven soldiers around her flying.

A wave of gravity following the attack pushed Father Todd's body forward.

Lily looked behind to see Father Todd trying to piece things together. Lily was just as surprised by what General Grey had said but the pieces did fit together. She had been defending the door when Father Todd woke up. Her mouth uncontrollably smiled when she remembered he went back inside for coffee before coming back out but when he did, he simply wiped a huge portion of the werewolf army from sight. She knew of no pastor who had that ability.

"That must be what they meant by he wasn't human. But which horseman is he?" she asked herself.

Captain Inertia and Kentro were quickly following behind them but Lily could see the werewolf army surging the shores again. There seemed to be no end to them in sight and Lily felt slightly relieved that they weren't the ones who had to face them.

Lily backed up for a second and then grabbed the other two, unfurling long white wings and flying upwards towards the ship. They landed on the deck of the ship but it was stark empty. Lily began to wonder why when she saw the little amount of crew that Captain Inertia had left was closely following him. They had all been in the battle with the elven warriors and they had all been able to hold their own. Now that the opportunity to leave the island unscathed was at hand, Captain Inertia had obviously ordered his men back to the ship. In turn, the elven army had begun to surge the beach from the other side and the werewolf army was caught in a pincer attack. The battle began to rage on as Lily helped the other two lower the walking bridge for when Captain Inertia, and his crew, got to the ship.

General Grey watched as the werewolves stood stunned on their ships, watching their comrades vanish into thin air. Only one creature had ever had that much power and it was called a Horseman by his mentor. His mentor never got the chance to expand on the issue because the Horseman led him into Demon Spawn and none of them had ever been seen again.

Father Todd came running past him and he couldn't help but feel that he was the Horseman. However, he didn't have the time to question him before the werewolves began charging at them once again.

"Form the ranks!" General Grey yelled.

Captain Inertia came running to his side, "You and the witches need to run."

General Grey looked at him and laughed, "I don't run. That's why I'm a Defense General. We're made to die in case we cannot defend an area."

"That's just stupid. Your enemy far outweighs you General, even if you are a two star," he said.

The two of them began to part the onslaught that came at them. Sarnia came falling from the sky like a meteor and crashed down in front of them. Captain Inertia raised his arm to shield himself from the blast. Captain Inertia felt his heart stop and words came whispering into his ear.

"Run little vampire."

Sarnia cracked her whip against the ground and time seemed to begin again. She licked her lips wickedly and her eyes were pointed directly at the two of them.

"Run, Inertia." General Grey stated gravely.

"That's death you're walking to elf," Captain Inertia said, relaxing his arms.

"I give my life up for your escape. Do not waste it vampire." General Grey said with a smile.

"Maybe we can live peacefully in the next life," Inertia said, placing his hand on the General's shoulder.

General Grey let out a heavy sigh before replying,

"Maybe. Take what you can."

Captain Inertia bolted into a run behind General Grey,

"And give no quarter!"

General Grey charged at Sarnia who began lashing her whip out on the ground, tossing soldiers left and right. He jumped into the air and brought down his fist into her face. The impact sent a sound wave throughout the island and the ground began to crack underneath the pressure.

General Grey began bashing her into the ground with his fists as the werewolves charged in around them, completely avoiding the dangerous area around Sarnia. Sarnia dodged his left hook finally and wrapped her whip around him.

Captain Inertia and his crew finally got to his ship when he realized that his cargo had made it aboard. They were even helping by placing the walk bridge down for them.

"Get those sails out. We make break now!" Captain Inertia called out to his men.

They set instantly to work to get the ship's sails out and the three of them pulled the bridge back in. Even though they were no longer at the brunt of the battle, it was still unbearably loud around them. Lily looked out over the battle towards Sarnia and her mouth showed a slight irritation as she watched the elven army begin to lose.

Father Todd was standing beside her and she felt an odd presence in the air. Then the sounds of snores came from his mouth. His body was glowing white again as the ship began to set sail. Father Todd got up on to the edge of the ship and jumped.

"Father Todd!" Lily yelled as she watched him jump in shock.

A white horse appeared on the waters below and she watched him charge off towards the island. The ship was gaining speed. Father Todd grew smaller and smaller, while Lily just fell back on to the deck of the ship.

"Meh, we'll meet again," she said hopefully.

In a sudden burst of light, an explosive sound wave hit the ship and Lily heard the sound of horse's hooves coming back towards the ship. A loud thud could be heard as Lily watched the General drop from the sky and the horse land on the ship. Father Todd fell to the ship unconscious.

"You could have at least caught them," Captain Inertia said as he stood over her.

"That would require effort and I was too busy last night to waste any," Lily stated bluntly.

"Busy doing what?" he asked.

"Heh, the stuff dreams are made of. Are we still taking the Moon river?" Lily asked.

"Yes but now we have General Grey aboard. We'll need to let the elven empire know that he came aboard unwillingly or else they'll bran him as a traitor." Captain Inertia pointed out.

"Now we have a horseman as well. It's going to be busy when we get to Heaven's Gate."

The three of them lay on the ground as the sky above them passed them by. Captain Inertia looked behind them at what was once an island and found that it had disappeared. He rushed down stairs to his chart cabin to see if it was truly gone. To his shock and disbelief, the entire island disappeared entirely off of his map.

"So he's that Horseman. This is turning out to be an interesting ride," Captain Inertia said as he walked back out of his chart cabin.

"Cannon fire!"

Meanwhile

"Sir, we have reports that a Horseman has been found!" An angel called from her desk.

"Do we know which one it is?" The head angel asked.

"No but we do know that Agent Lily Trotter will be bringing him here."

"Do we have the reception ready at the Academy of Magic?"

"Yes but there are some complications."

"What complications?"

"An enemy is within the mage's ranks."

"Who?"

"It's…"

Back to the ship

"Captain Inertia, the pirates are attacking us from the front. At our speed, we'll collide into the enemy ship," Kentro said.

"Hard port right, it looks like we're headed to the Blood Styx boys. Ready the arc cannons for immediate departure," Captain Inertia replied.

Father Todd woke up to see a glaring sun looking straight back at him as he lay on the deck of the ship. The sway of the ship and the spray of the oceanic seemed peaceful until the breeze stopped for a moment. Then Father Todd came to realize just how wet his body was with the death-bringing humidity crushing in on his lungs.

Father Todd yanked himself from the deck of the ship and sat in wonder as he saw nothing but sky around them. Sure, there were trees and spotty bits of land every few feet, but most of the *river* was more of an open ocean.

He struggled to his feet and wobbled over to the side of the ship. His eyes were jerked wide open as the river itself looked as if it were blood instead of water. The sight of it made him sick to his stomach and a big hand patted his back.

"That's how nearly everyone reacts to the Blood Styx river if they have never been to it before." A friendly voice with the sound of many years spoke to him from behind, "The elves simply called it Blood Styx until the human addition of river came to be common. It's still titled Blood Styx on our maps though."

Father Todd turned his head to see General Grey standing next to him with a smile of wisdom.

"What is that colour?" Father Todd asked.

General Grey looked overboard at the water, as if examining it, before replying, "The base of the river and the ground underneath it are made of red dirt. The trees that we've passed by are oil sap trees that excrete oil as a way to deterrent any plant eaters. The oil mixes in with the bright red water to lighten the colour and make it seem thicker since oil mixed with water makes water heavier."

"Wow. Here I was thinking that everything involved magic of some sort," Father Todd said with a nervous smile.

"Well, if it makes you feel any better, people used to say that this river belonged to those who fought forever in hell. Then if you were the reason why a war was started, that you would be sent to hell to fight others like yourself for all eternity. The blood would be so much that it came up at the top of Blood Styx Mountain and poured on to the Earth." General Grey said before bursting out in laughter, "Then again, that'd require one hell of a twisted mind to think up."

"Father Todd, can you please come with me?" Lily's voice asked from afar.

Father Todd turned to see Lily standing in the doorway, waiting for him to follow her. She waited until he got to her before going down deeper into the ship. There was an awkward silence between the two as they made their way past the other cabins and into the map room. Captain Inertia was sitting there already, waiting for the two of them to arrive.

Before Father Todd began to say anything, Lily interrupted, "Now, what I know of is the last locations of the four Shadow Ghosts. Provided they haven't been moved, they are all in separate locations and most likely in the centre of massacred village or city. Except for one and that's because one particular Shadow Ghost made their way into Demon Spawn. Perhaps to hide from the enemy in plain sight or just out of foolish reasons."

"Where are the other three?" Captain Inertia asked.

"One is at the foot of Heaven's Gate and the other two are located inside of villages," Lily stated bluntly, "Now, we will use the Academy of Magic's knowledge of magic bottles to see if there has already been a spell used on Sarnia's bottles that has worked in the past. However…"

"Which villages?" Captain Inertia interrupted with a malcontented smile.

Lily glared at him, "You know what villages."

"Yes, but the good pastor here should know."

Lily made a laboured sigh and walked over to Father Todd, whom was now sitting in his chair. She grabbed his hands and struggled to answer.

"We don't know where the second one is but the very first Shadow Ghost to be captured was in your village."

Father Todd's body simply froze as he thought back to all the people he had known in the village.

"We don't know what name it went under but reports have it that it was helping out the community their by providing cakes."

Father Todd's eyes looked into hers, "I know who it is…I know where they live…I've known them almost all of my life."

Lily nodded sympathetically but then paused for a moment more, "However, that will be the last one to be freed."

Father Todd's eyes scrunched in confusion, "Why? My village is stark empty. There's no one there."

"Captain Inertia was the last ship leaving that island before the werewolves made a final attack and claimed it as their territory," Lily stated, "It's now crawling with the beasts and getting inside of it will be even more difficult than getting into Demon Spawn. Demon Spawn have holes of unguarded territory in their land because they are a main land, the Island of Misery has no such holes."

"You know what Lily? This is all well and good, but if this man will be travelling with us then me and him need to do something," Captain Inertia said, getting up from his chair.

"You will listen to me captain…" Lily began.

"No, you will listen to me *cargo*. This boy needs to know how to use a weapon or else he'll get us killed. He needs to know more than fancy white magic if he is to survive," Captain Inertia said, "And I'll be damned to die because I refused to teach him such things."

Captain Inertia grabbed Father Todd by his collar and began pulling him out of the room. Father Todd begged with his face to Lily to free him but Lily just gave him a smile, shaking her head. They made their way to the deck and Captain Inertia threw him out of the doorway, and on to the ground. He also pulled out his sword and chucked it at him.

The crew began to gather around but Captain Inertia gave them a glare and yelled, "Back to work swabs or I'll be having fresh dinner tonight."

Captain Inertia held his sword out to the side of the boat and said, "I call forth Orepeal of the river. Come demon, do my bidding."

Silence wrung among the ship as everyone waited to see what would happen. Suddenly, a red hand with no finely formed shape grabbed on to the ledge of the side, pulling up a creature made out of the water. Several similar creatures started pouring on to the ship.

"We will now begin a trial and error session to successfully train you. Until we get to the Academy of Magic, these creatures will not stop attacking you. They *will* kill you if given the chance and they are extremely fast, given that they will fall apart with a successful hit."

The blood demons began charging at Father Todd, who froze in place as their movements began to slow down. At first, Father Todd was filled with fear and he was absolutely certain that he would die but then he felt a small bit of warmth coming from his hand. Without thinking, he dropped the sword back to the floor of the ship and placed the free hand on top of book.

Captain Inertia watched Father Todd to the moment that he placed his hand on the book. Father Todd seemed to have frozen again and when Captain Inertia placed his foot forward to jump in the fight, his eyes felt extremely strained as they caught up to the pastor's speed. In a flash of light, every blood demon that had climbed on the ship burst into puddles of water as Father Todd slashed through them with his blinding white scythe. The pastor's eyes leaked white light and Captain Inertia's mouth dropped as he saw the pastor's horse buck into the air.

"What have I brought on my ship?" was all that Captain Inertia could ask.

Just as soon as it had happened, the blinding white light blinked out of existence and Father Todd collapsed on the ground again. However, he struggled to his feet and felt the warmth surge through his body.

Captain Inertia began to realize why Father Todd hadn't passed out this time as the vampire watched the blood demons continue to surge their way on top of the ship.

"Helmsman, get this ship out of the river!" Captain Inertia yelled in a panic.

"Sorry, Captain, we've got yet another half mile before we hit the Tower of Supreme!" the helmsman yelled.

A hand came on to Captain Inertia's should and he looked behind himself to see Lily standing there.

"I will take care of this," Lily stated.

Lily walked forward, crouched down, and bit her finger, wiping it in a circle around her on the deck at her feet.

"Damned right of the flame, let my anger unleash and not tame," Lily said as she marked her forehead with the same blood.

The air around them began to vibrate for a second and in one blast, gravity crushed everyone to the ground. Many of the crew were sent through the floor of the ship. Lily's wings expanded out of the back of her overcoat and she flew into the air in a straight line above the circle. Every inch she climbed in the air was another blast of even more gravity.

Her body spun in the air and spears of blood were sent flying in every direction, aiming for every demon that was climbing on the ship.

"Land Ho! The tower is just ahead!" The man from the bird's perch called out.

The tower itself came into view a few moments later but Captain Inertia was now more preoccupied with Father Todd, who was calmly walking towards him. The book in his hand was glowing pure white to the point that the book was no longer visible.

"Father Todd!" Captain Inertia yelled.

Father Todd had no reaction and the scythe he had held before was slowly reappearing in his hand.

"Father Todd! Wake up!" Captain Inertia screamed at the pastor.

Captain Inertia bolted towards him with his claws drawn and in a moment's time, he saw the scythe slice downwards. Captain Inertia stopped dead in his tracks and felt a weird sensation in his body. Then he began to fall towards the ground but when he tried to catch himself with his hands, he saw that his entire body had been cut into cubes.

In a burst of red mist, Captain Inertia surrounded Father Todd and was inches away from his throat when he felt his body solidify once again. The next thing he knew, his body was flying through the air to the end of the ship, and Father Todd's was being sent in the other direction. Lily had landed in the spot that they were at and both of her hands had extended. She had shoved them apart.

The crew could not see what was happening and only Captain Inertia was able to keep up with the speed. Lily was already being attacked by Father Todd, who swung his scythe aimlessly at Lily. With each crash of the blade on her skin, the deck was cut by the sheer impact. Lily grabbed Father Todd's scythe arm and his cuff link, slamming her head into his.

The collision hit the mast behind them causing it to slowly fall to the side of the ship.

Lily threw Father Todd aside as the remaining blood demons began to bombard the ship endlessly. In a blinding flurry, Lily shot bolts of lightning from her hands to each of the demons. With the final shot, the ship lurched forward as it bumped against the docking grounds. They had reached the Tower of Supreme but the ship was in more of a wreck than it had been when it arrived at its previous location.

Lily brought her wings back into her overcoat, quickly walking over to Captain Inertia who was sitting on the ground with his mouth wide open.

"You do not give a horseman a life or death choice," Lily stated as she swiftly walked past him to the cabin area, "It will always end in death."

Father Todd lay on the ground in a heap of unconsciousness once again as footsteps passed him. Captain Inertia watched with disgust as the Knighthood unit came up to them with their leader in front. Captain Inertia smacked away the hand that the leader gave to help him on his feet. Once he was standing, Captain Inertia looked her in the eyes.

"I do not deal with your kind." He stated.

She smiled at him sympathetically with a following nod.

"Welcome to the Academy of Magic. I will be your guide while you stay," Cassimpra said.

Lily and Captain Inertia found them sharing ideas about to kill her with their hands as Cassimpra led them to the centre of the Tower of Supreme.

"As I said, welcome to the Academy of Magic. I know you two are authorized members to the Academy but the rest of your crew, including the pastor, will need to stay in the guest room until you are done with your business here." Cassimpra said, "We will need to go across the Bridge of Eternity." Cassimpra led them to the door at the back of the tower as Captain Inertia nodded his men to follow the Knighthood.

Father Todd and Canting were being carried by Kentro as Lily watched them leave.

"Now, before we come across the bridge, I am required to ask what your business is here at the Academy." Cassimpra stated.

"I am here to gain access to Heaven's Gate," Captain Inertia said with a nod.

"I am here for various reasons under the authority of Heaven," Lily said with her arms crossed. "Care to elaborate?" Cassimpra asked.

"Spirits of Ennui, if you do not let me cross this bridge then you will suffer what I can do to your way of life," Lily said as she looked up into the air at what seemed to be nothing to Captain Inertia.

Cassimpra frowned, "Threats are not taken kindly to here."

"My patience does not exist, traitorous vampire." Lily bluntly pointed out.

"Fine, then let us begin the walk." Cassimpra stated.

The door opened to the bridge on the other side, which was entirely made of blue crystal. They began to walk across the bridge and magic letters began to appear in the air above them.

What is the most sacred thing in the world?

"Your soul," all three stated.

Around half way over the bridge, another set of magic letters began to appear.

What will kill you?

"The reluctance of failure."

The final set of magic letters appeared as a gate of fire.

What is forbidden?

"Everything."

Captain Inertia followed behind them quietly as the three of them travelled through the hallway.

"Have you found your father yet?" Lily asked.

"Why do you ask?" Cassimpra snidely rebuked.

"You're my sister."

"You denied me the easiest way to find him, so no."

The tension between the two was slightly intoxicating but they made their way to the council room door. Cassimpra turned to them and pointed at Lily.

"You will go first. Only one person may enter this chamber at a time." Cassimpra pointed out as she turned her gaze from Lily to Captain Inertia, "Which means that you and I will need to stay here and wait for them. They will let me know when they are ready and we will not know when Lily leaves the room as all entries are given a different area to leave from for safety measures."

Cassimpra opened the doors to the council room and Lily walked in slowly. The room was dark except for six blue candles that stood on separate pedestals in the room. The air inside the room was fresh and clean, unlike the Academy, and it smelled of fresh flowers. Lily always found this odd about the council room but she put it out of her mind.

"What is she here for?" The Spirits of Ennui asked.

Lily peered into the darkness only to find that she couldn't see a thing.

"What is she wanting? All this fuss over a little medallion and she comes to us, what is she here for?" The Spirits of Ennui asked again.

"I am here to request passage to Heaven's Gate on two mortals' behalf. His presence has been requested in Heaven's Gate," Lily stated.

"But there is no mortal that travels with you?" The Spirits of Ennui asked, sounding puzzled by the request.

"There is a pastor named Todd and a tree goblin named Canting that travels with me," Lily stated.

"These are not mortals, incompetent detective. Yes, incompetent detective."

"I have recently discovered that the pastor may be the vessel of a horseman. Otherwise, these two are very mortal, I assure you," Lily stated, crossing her arms in irritation.

"She does not know, she does not know. She travels, she sees, and yet she does not know. How does she not know?" The Spirits of Ennui taunted.

"Listen, you know who I am talking about, just give them passage."

"You must know, that the pastor is neither mortal nor horseman. Do you still request passage?" The Spirits of Ennui asked.

"Yes. He is going to Heaven's Gate so that we can find out who he is."

"Heaven knows, heaven knows. They know but keep silent, as so many things they do. They may have passage but he will be one you need to seek eventually," The Spirits of Ennui stated.

"He can command the white magic in a deadly manner. Only a horseman can do such a thing."

"There are many more. She is wrong, she is wrong. Oh how wrong she is. She doesn't even know what the creature is hiding, no one knows except the Spirits of Ennui." The Spirits of Ennui said.

"What is ... the creature hiding?" Lily asked.

Lily did not find cryptic information very fun to deal with but the overall tale of what she needed to do may reside in their answers. Her mind frantically tried to piece together what they could have meant about Father Todd but it seemed as though she would find out what he was at some point in time. She could feel that the Spirits of Ennui were anxious and maybe even excited to know that they knew something about Canting that she did not.

Up until this point, Lily did find it strange that Canting was alone. Tree goblins were normally stupid and travelled in packs, with little to no intelligence inside of their skulls. Yet Canting showed a remarkable intellect for poems, magic, and the world in general. It was always a surprise to see how far Canting's knowledge was and the idea that there was an intelligent tree goblin in the world nagged at her mind.

"What of the captain? Yes, what of the captain? Does he have a passage already?" The Spirits of Ennui asked.

"He will ask of his own accord. I will not be responsible for his actions," Lily pointed out.

"They may all have passage. Now leave us." The Spirits of Ennui said abruptly.

"But… but what about what the creature is hiding?" Lily asked.

"Yes, about that – about that indeed. We have your answer but you need to dig. The foundations of earth comes from the words of one, scrawled on metal not of this world, how does the tree speak of years beyond its roots if it has not a thing to hide among its branches. Now, be gone. Seek another truth that has been hidden by Heaven," The Spirits of Ennui said.

Lily found herself falling from the sky and she groaned as her body fell softly on to the grass.

"Stupid spirits, things go smoother if you just tell me," she said.

"Yes, but they find it fun to run in circles around others. I would too if I had access to all the knowledge in the universe." A familiar voice said.

Kentro was sitting next to her as she looked over to him. His eyes looked red, as if he had been crying for some time and Lily noticed that he was sad but not depressed. Following his eyes, she turned her head to see a grave marker in front of them. It was the grave of her mother.

"She was a wonderful woman," Kentro said.

"I know, she was my mother," Lily stated.

"No, you have no idea what your mother did outside of Heaven's Gate. It's truly a marvel how one angel can help so many people."

"She was an angel, Dad, it's what they do."

"I remember the day I saw her, I was standing in front of the mayor's office. She had just gotten done with explaining how my complaints were relevant to the town and that the mayor needed to prepare for an attack. Your mother had heard my prayers and had come to my aid. I walked into the office without even realizing what she had done and the mayor laid out his plan for my approval of the town's defenses. Sure, we were still attacked but almost everyone survived the attack, which only happened a week later," Kentro said, the tears beginning to form up in his eyes again, "I miss her, she's a wonderful woman."

There was silence between them as Kentro cried over the grave and Lily patiently waited for him to stop crying. She found it remarkably hilarious inside of her head to see a fur ball of death cry. Lily knew it might have been cruel but the two were opposites to her.

"What do you mean by *is*?" Lily asked gravely.

Kentro froze in place for a moment, looking at Lily as his brain processed her question.

"What do you mean? Did I say *is*?" Kentro asked nervously.

"Yes Kentro, you said *is*," Lily stated, "*Is* implies that this grave is fake. Is that what the Spirits of Ennui meant by *another truth hidden by Heaven*? Were you told to keep my mother's death believable?"

Kentro looked at her uncomfortably for a moment and then shrugged.

"Dad, you need to be honest with me. Are you hiding the fact that my mother is still alive?" Lily asked.

Kentro shook his head.

"*Daaad,*" *Lily said* with emphasis on her glaring eyes.

"It's not a fact, it's a maybe." Kentro pointed out quickly. "She may be alive? How do you not know?" Lily asked.

"Her last mission was to hide the fact that Cassimpra was the daughter of the Shadow Master that knew where the Medal of Scalon was hidden. This meant that your mother needed to recover all traces of where the two had interacted in the past and do several UN-angelic things. Memory wiping mostly, which did a lot of emotional and mental damage," Kentro said, "Now, while she was on one of those tracks that she had found, she just disappeared. The recovery team never found a body and they found an entire village covered in death. Instead of marking the fact that such a highly esteemed angel could have become a fallen, they just proclaimed her dead. Something that's more than a *little* unbelievable."

"Angels can die dad. I know you don't see the way of the angelic life to often but they're not immortal," Lily said.

Kentro shook his head, "Your mother was a pure angel. The vampire blood in her body had been rejected by her body. That was what she told me the last time I had seen her."

Two troubling facts had just boiled to the surface; A pure angel was, indeed, immortal as it's the one angel made of pure light and Lily had never heard of a vampire's blood being rejected from a body. If this was so and her mother was still alive, then why had she become a fallen. Even more troubling is that fallen angels often leave obvious trails because they're not used to being fallen at first, but her mother had just disappeared. This meant she was still in the village at the time and the recovery team looked over a possible possession.

"Was there a survivor in that village?"

"I don't know. I've tried to find out what I could but the rest of it is inside Heaven Gate's file department," Kentro said with a shrug, "You could probably find out though."

"Every time I think I have the answer, I find more secrets that have been hidden from me come to the surface." Lily finished with frustration as she got up and stormed back into the Academy of Magic.

Lily walked back to Captain Inertia who was standing in front of the council room door still. Cassimpra was no longer there, which gave Lily a slight relief.

"Captain Inertia, after Heaven's Gate, will you still be willing to transport Father Todd?" Lily asked.

Captain Inertia looked at Lily for a moment before replying with a question, "Do you believe he'll be vital in doing what we need to do?"

"I believe he might be part of what we need to do but we still have no idea what he is. If what happened on the ship is any indication of what could happen, I wanted to get your scope on the risk assessment of this," Lily stated.

"I'm a pirate. Everything I do is a risk. I'm trying to keep being a pirate and if that means that I need to have some freaks aboard my ship, then let me show them the walkway. The true question here is whether *you* can trust him or not." Captain Inertia pointed out.

"He doesn't even know who he is."

"Simply an adventure by itself for Father Todd. He's not important in this though, you are. You've been designated by Heaven *and* Hell to, essentially, fix the world. All this talk is making my mouth dry."

Captain Inertia pulled out his flask and took a quick swig from it, coughing as the liquid burned in his throat. Lily frowned but she expected it out of pirates and she waited for him to start talking again.

"Like I said, you're the detective in all of this. You tell me where to go and Father Todd is following you," Captain Inertia stated, "But I will say this. A possible horseman, a tree goblin, an Angelic Detective, and an elven general, all on one boat going into the most dangerous environments on Earth. This is going to be one hell of a time."

Lily smiled at Captain Inertia, "You always have a way with words."

"That's because words have a way with women and I've met a lot of..."

Lily interrupted him, "No, just no."

Lily opened the door for Captain Inertia and they both walked into the room.

Captain Inertia looked at her, "Didn't Cassimpra say..."

Lily just shook her head and Captain Inertia fell silent. The room was different this time. Instead of blue with candles around the room, there was a red liquid that floated around the room in a circle. The light in the room was a warm red that reflected light out of the liquid.

"She has broken the rules."

"You have broken my patience."

"You need to follow our rules, you are not excusable." The Spirits of Ennui said in irritation.

"You needed to answer my questions but you decided to have fun with it didn't you?"

"Yes, yes we did. Were we supposed to say that? Do we care?" The Spirits of Ennui asked.

"Listen, I need the pass. Just give me the pass," Captain Inertia stated.

"Little vampire needs to learn his place." The Spirits of Ennui said.

"You know what I don't need is this crap. Heaven's Gate wants me to come to their place then they can open the door.

I'm not dealing with people who are already dead who get a kick out of goading people who are still alive," Captain Inertia said as he left the room.

"You see what you did? You guys are one of the main sources of information and guidance in the universe. Yet... you guys are just nothing more than elegant highwaymen," Lily said as she left after him.

"We will see you again detective. Will you have saved the world or will you stand beside us in the prison of the abyss?" The Spirits of Ennui asked.

Lily bent her hat down and closed the door behind her.

Meanwhile

Father Todd awoke to a severe pain in his head and he grabbed it with both of his hands. It was one of the worst headaches that he's ever had. As the pain slowly began to pass by, his eyes began to accustom themselves to the room. It was a rather nice room that had a similar surrounding to what he had expected to see where he used to live.

Around him, he saw large beings in full armour. Father Todd stood up and looked inside the armour; there was nothing there.

"Is there something on my face?" A deep voice asked.

Father Todd whipped his head around and then realized that he had been looking directly to where a face would be inside the armour. He extended a finger and poked something inside the armour.

"Ah!" Father Todd screamed.

The two pieces of armour began to laugh hard.

"What are you?"

"We are called the Knighthood." It said.

Father Todd shook his hand and extended his hand, "I'm sorry, I'm still learning. Will you accept this apology?"

"There's no need to apologize. We see this quite a bit here at the Academy." It said.

"May I see the Academy?" Father Todd asked.

The two pieces of armour shrugged, "Don't see why not.

You seem harmless enough."

A few minutes later

"You know, there's a lot of neat things here but for an Academy for one of the most powerful tools on the planet. You don't seem to have a lot of students." Father Todd pointed out.

One of the Knighthood laughed, "I like you. You seem like a simple guy. Of course you don't see anyone on the surface; this is where the first years come. Once you can pass the test of magic, that's when you're enrolled into the school below.

Many of them die down there."

"Why is that?"

"The school has a learn at your own pace policy, even though there are spirits for teachers. The ones that have left believe that they have learned what they've needed from magic and that it's time to live life on the surface again. There's a level for every strength of magic, so around the fiftieth floor most people come back up."

"How many floors are there?"

"It's not a measurable number."

"Oh, have there been parts that have collapsed?"

"No, it's just that no one has ever made it down to the bottom and lived. Even still, there is only one Shadow Master who made it to the bottom but he did not count the amount of floors he went down. His name is Leyster Sandwak and he was once our beloved Cassimpra's father." The armour said.

Father Todd began to speak but the sets of armour held up their hands to silence him. He could hear what sounded like scraping. A few feet from them, men were climbing up on to the walkway of the Academy.

"Werewolves, warn the others." One set of armour said to the other.

The other set of armour picked Father Todd up and threw him on his back. They began to run back towards the Tower of Supreme when Father Todd saw Captain Inertia and Lily talking. He cupped his hands together and yelled over to them.

"Werewolves!" Father Todd yelled.

The two of them heard him and began running towards them. After a few seconds, they managed to catch up behind him.

"Why is a member of the Knighthood carrying you like a damsel in distress?" Lily asked.

Father Todd began to speak before the set of armour burst out, "I could tell by the way he held himself that he's essentially useless in a fight."

The two of them tried to hold it in but they couldn't and Father Todd's shot down feelings were thrown out the window as Captain Inertia and Lily began laughing wildly.

"I don't appreciate that." Father Todd muffled.

As they came up to the bridge, Father Todd felt himself being lowered towards the ground. He was grateful at first because the ride was beginning to make him sick. Then he turned around and saw what was charging at fully speed on the Bridge of Eternity.

"Okay you three, I want a standard formation. Angel and Vampire protect the mage while I clear a path." The set of armour stated.

Lily and Captain Inertia nodded. Father Todd slumped down in depression as lamented over having to surge through yet another fight. The three of them slowly made their way across the bridge carefully. Lily was guarding Father Todd from the back as Captain Inertia was kicking the ones trying to climb up off the sides again. The werewolves piled in but the three of them act as a barrier shield, simply tossing the werewolves off the bridge and into the river.

"How are the werewolves not being affected?" Father Todd asked Captain Inertia.

"Mortals are not seen as a threat by the bridge, so they can simply walk through," Captain Inertia said.

"How would army be stopped from coming in?"

"That's what Cassimpra and the Knighthood are for. Cassimpra guards the Academy halls because she can use magic while the Knighthood protects the magic-nullify zone. The Blood Demons that you saw before is a rite of passage; I just acted as if I was summoning a demon to terrify you." Captain Inertia explained as he continued to kick the werewolves off the side of the bridge, "Technically, the werewolf was the only flaw in the design. However, they'll never get down to the first floor of the Academy because the spirit teachers will wipe them out in case Cassimpra isn't enough."

They finally made it to the door to the Tower of Supreme and upon opening it, they were hard pressed to think they could get through without getting in a scrape. They struggled a few feet before the werewolves began separating them. Father Todd began to summon the magic from his book before Kentro jumped in and began shoving the enemy off.

"Get to the door, the crew is waiting for you." Kentro yelled.

Father Todd made their way to the door and waited for the other three to fall in. Kentro protected their backs as they ran out the door but as he himself came out, there was a distinct sound of a swishing noise. They all turned back to see that Kentro's head had been ripped off.

"No!" Lily screamed as she began to run back towards the werewolves.

Father Todd yanked back around and joined Captain Inertia as they fought Lily from going back into the battle. In a burst of energy and debris, the Tower of Supreme's walls fell in upon themselves. The werewolves inside ignored the Knighthood that had been fending them off and began to charge at *The Vile Jewel* in full speed.

A black mist formed around them and another squad of the Knighthood took the werewolves head on with Cassimpra leading the charge. The crew threw the bridge board down for them as they came close and Father Todd struggled with Captain Inertia to force her on the ship.

"Go, leave now!" Cassimpra yelled.

Lily ran to the side of the ship, "What about you?!"

"I'll be fine, just go, just…"

Lily screamed as she saw what happened next and fell to her knees in despair. Cassimpra stood there as she looked down to see blood coming out from her chest. Then in a moment of realization, she realized that she made a mistake.

"Oh."

Her final word as her lifeless body fell into the river to be devoured by the Blood Demons. Father Todd turned to Captain Inertia, whose mouth was still wide open from shock, and yelled questions at him.

"Why didn't she mist? Why didn't she escape the way normal vampires escape? What happened?"

Captain Inertia slowly turned to him as the ship set sail on the river and further out to the sea. His words hit Father Todd hard.

"Magic is nullified when you step on the grounds of the Tower of Supreme," he said, his voice shaking, "She was no different than a human right then."

Father Todd sunk to the floor next to Lily, who was still crying as hard as her body would let her. He wrapped his arms around her and began crying with her. For a time, there was silence on the ship, even among the crew. Father Todd noticed at that moment that the crew had always talked during moments of silence and it had always a comfortable reprieve.

Kentro and Cassimpra were now dead. General Grey was nowhere to be found aboard the deck of the ship. Canting had gone missing during this time and the most powerful warrior on the ship was now in tears. The rain began to fall as they made their way out to sea and it drenched them all.

Lily stopped crying for a moment and looked up into the clouds. Her face red from the misery her body was going through.

"Hello all." Something said.

Father Todd looked around to see who had said it but could find no one. Then his shadow began to rise out of the ground and formed the shape of a man. It stood there, towering above like a menacing monster.

"I am Leyster Sandwak," it said.

Lily's eyes widened as she said with hardly any breath left inside of her, "The Shadow Master."

About the Author

Mark Peter Evans is a writer who mainly works with performance. By focusing on techniques and materials, Evans tries to focus on the activity of presenting. The character, shape or content of the presented writing is secondary. The essential things are the momentary and the intention of presenting. His performances appear as dreamlike images in which fiction and reality meet, well-known tropes merge, meanings shift, past and present fuse. Time and memory always play a key role. By applying a poetic and often metaphorical language, he wants to amplify the astonishment of the spectator by creating compositions or settings that generate tranquil poetic images that leave traces and balances on the edge of recognition and alienation. His works are notable for their perfect finish and tactile nature. This is of great importance and bears witness to great craftsmanship. By replaying the work for each exhibition and pushing the evocative power of the work a little further, he considers making writing a craft which is executed using clear formal rules and which should always refer to social reality. His works are presented with the aim not to provide an idealistic view but to identify where light and the environment are important. The energy of a place and its emotional and spiritual vibrations are always important. Mark was born in 1969 in the town of Wrexham, North Wales, United Kingdom, and spent his childhood living and growing up in the village of Afoneitha. Mark attended Penycae and Grango school Rhos Wrexham. Mark started writing from an early age. He first knew he could write after being commended by his English teacher at the age of thirteen for the short story he had written. However, the author decided to work full time and leave his writing career until he felt the time was right. His claim to fame was with Sir Tim Rice many years ago when he sent some material for some feedback. Mark recently got married to his wife Julie. They both live in Jersey, Channel Isles. Mark Currently works for Waitrose, part of the John Lewis Partnership. Mark enjoys spending time with family, visiting family in stunning North Wales, listening to all sorts of music, relaxing when he is not writing. Mark also enjoys beach walks and enjoying the fantastic scenery that the island of Jersey has to offer.